This edition first published 2017 by Fahrenheit Press

10 9 8 7 6 5 4 3 2 1

www.Fahrenheit-Press.com

F 4 E

Blackwater

By

GJ Moffat

Fahrenheit Press

For The Fam.

1

Deputy Sheriff Early Simms inherited his size from his father, Charlie. He was six foot three in his bare feet and weighed over two hundred and twenty pounds, most of it muscle. At thirty-five, Early had done a fine job of keeping himself in shape though he had not played football since he was a week short of his eighteenth birthday. His stomach wasn't as flat as it used to be but he did his best to keep it in check, running three miles most mornings and lifting weights a couple of times a week.

Early walked out of the hot August sun and into the reception area of the Silver Dunes retirement home. He recognised the woman at the front desk from previous visits but could not recall her name. She was dressed in a soft, pastel uniform.

'Morning Mr Simms,' she said. 'Another beautiful day.'

'Sure enough,' Early said, taking off his Blackwater Sheriff's Department baseball cap and wiping sweat up through his hair with his hand.

He still had most of his hair, though it had darkened as he grew older to what his mother used to call dirty blond. It was cut short and pressed flat on his head from the baseball cap. It stood up at the front where he had wiped at the sweat.

'My dad awake yet?'

The woman smiled.

'You know that he's always first up, now, don't you.'

'Old habits.'

Charlie Simms had been Blackwater's Sheriff for over thirty years. He was still working at sixty-four when disease started to eat at his brain. Early could see the pain in his father's eyes as he searched his son's face, desperately trying to remember the man in front of him, trying to place him from somewhere in his life. Most of the time he failed.

Early's mother, Tabitha, had died eight years ago. She hadn't lived to see her husband become less than the man he used to be. Early was thankful for that.

He walked past the front desk and along a short corridor to the sunroom at the side of the home. It was glass fronted and looked out over a well-tended lawn that ended at a high, wooden fence. A gardener in faded jeans and a khaki shirt with the sleeves rolled up to his elbows kneeled beside a flowerbed and dug at the loose earth.

A male attendant came into the room behind Early and took a plate of scrambled eggs to a woman seated alone by the west window. The attendant put a fork in the woman's hand and said something encouraging to her in a low voice. The woman smiled at him.

The only other resident in the room was Charlie Simms. He sat upright in his chair with his fine, grey hair neatly combed and his dressing gown firmly tied at the waist. Early walked to his father and put his hand on the man's neck, feeling short stubble there. He leaned down and kissed his father's forehead before sitting opposite him.

'Had a haircut, Dad?' Early asked.

His father looked at the stranger sitting at his table.

'My son usually comes to see me for breakfast on Tuesday,' he said.

'It is Tuesday, Dad.'

Confusion passed across Charlie's face and he glanced out of the window at the gardener, ashamed by his inability to understand what this man was talking about. He knew it wasn't Tuesday yet. If it were Tuesday, his son would be here.

Early covered his mouth with a hand and breathed in through his nose, afraid that his father would see the flesh of his chin tremble.

'He always comes Tuesday,' Charlie said. 'My boy, Early.'

His father turned to face him again, the sense of certainty returning to his face.

'Plays football. Going to turn professional and be a big star they say. I tell him he's got to graduate high school first. Education is important.'

Early nodded. He'd heard this story before – lived it twenty years ago.

'Best linebacker they ever saw,' Charlie Simms went on. 'That's what the college scouts tell me.'

Early saw his father's eyes light up for a moment, the man he used to be fighting to resurface.

'Do you know what they say about him?' Charlie asked the boy that used to play football.

'No, what's that?'

Charlie Simms shook his head. A tear squeezed out the corner of his left eye. Early picked up a paper napkin and leaned across the table to wipe it away.

'Hits like a freight train,' Early said, finishing the thought for his father.

'He'll get over it, you know.'

Early froze, his hand a few inches from his father's face.

'That boy was too small to be playing, anyway. My son, Early, was just doing his job. Hit him hard and clean.'

The memory of a sound echoed in Early's head – the sound of a boy's neck breaking. But that wasn't the worst of it. No, it was the last breath the boy took as Early kneeled beside him, holding his hand. The breath shivered and crackled in his throat as he blinked and tears ran off his face into his hair as he lay on the dusty field.

Early wiped his father's face and sat heavily in the chair.

'Hasn't played in a month since it happened,' Charlie said. 'He'll play again, won't he? My son, I mean.'

Early knew that the answer was no.

'I'm sure that he will, sir,' was what he said.

The old man smiled again and went back to watching the gardener. Early got up and left, placing a hand on his father's shoulder as he passed.

Outside, Early put his cap on and leaned against the metal of his department Ford. It was white with the green livery of the sheriff's department. He bowed his head and felt the heat of the sun on the back of his neck.

He used to think that if he wished it hard enough, that boy would still be alive. That if he closed his eyes real tight he could resurrect him by sheer force of will alone.

But he was still dead after all this time.

And Early never forgot what death sounded like.

2

Kennedy's diner sat at the east end of Main Street, Blackwater – too far along the town's main thoroughfare for many tourists to get there. The owner, Pat Kennedy, never had a good word to say about his bank; and less than that to say about tourists. Early Simms had breakfast there every Tuesday after he visited Silver Dunes to tell Pat how his dad was doing. Pat had gone to school with Charlie Simms.

Early drove his car along Reunion Highway with the driver's window open and his arm resting on the door, the hairs on his arm ruffled by the passing air. The skin of his arms was deeply tanned, a result of his preference for short-sleeved shirts in the summer months. There was no wind today and the temperature was already at seventy. It wasn't nine yet. Early tapped his hand on the steering wheel to the sound of the Black Crowes' 'Remedy' as it played on the local radio station.

He turned onto Main Street and passed the Baptist church on the green, continuing past the town hall on the right and watching as the storeowners went about getting ready for the day's trade. He raised a hand in greeting to those that saw him. He got smiles, waves and even a 'Howdy' in return. He liked howdy. It was a word people didn't use enough any more. It was one of his dad's old standards.

The sheriff's office where he spent most of his days was a mile along the street on the left – a single storey wooden building painted white with a flagpole in the middle of a narrow strip of lawn. A stars and stripes hung unenthusiastically from the top of the flagpole, undisturbed in the summer heat.

Early pulled the car to a stop beside the office and walked across the street towards Kennedy's, hitching his belt up and resting his right hand on the butt of the nine-millimetre pistol holstered on his hip. A fortyish couple reached the diner ahead of him. They were swinging a six-year-old girl between them, the man wearing a hat with 'Wicked Pissah' printed on it that he must have bought at one of the tourist traps in town earlier in the week. A teenage boy followed them, his head bowed and moving in time with whatever was blasting through the headphones that were clamped over his ears. He glanced at Early, quickened his step and followed his parents inside.

There was an old-fashioned brass bell above the door. It rang when anyone walked in. Pat Kennedy was behind a wooden counter that ran the length of the left-hand wall of the diner. He was pouring a cup of coffee for one of his buddies, Riley Shurmur. Kennedy nodded at Early and motioned for him to sit beside Shurmur. Early wasn't too fond of the man. He smelled of stale beer and BO on his best days. Kennedy ignored the tourist couple. They looked unsure of the place and spoke in quiet English accents. Early wasn't surprised. The diner was well worn and comfortable for locals. Nothing fancy. The tourists looked like they were used to better in their Ralph Lauren summer wardrobe.

'It doesn't look like much,' Early said, smiling at the little girl. 'But the food's real good.'

The woman returned his smile uncertainly. Early touched the peak of his cap for good measure. He wanted to say 'Ma'am', but resisted; sometimes you could go too far.

He sat at the counter, two seats away from Shurmur who was dressed in a dirty pair of blue work pants and what was once a white t-shirt. Shurmur scratched at his beard and stared at Early.

'Mornin', Riley,' Early said, taking his cap off and putting it on the counter.

Shurmur stared at him for a moment with rheumy eyes before going back to his coffee.

Kennedy walked to where Early sat and filled his cup with coffee. He was a small man, no more than five foot five, and his hair had long since gone. His skin was wrinkled from exposure to the sun and a pipe smoking habit he had picked up in his early thirties.

'How's your dad?' Kennedy asked.

Early raised the cup and took a sip.

'Not so good today, you know.'

Kennedy pursed his lips and looked out onto the street through the front window.

'Life's a bitch.'

'You're not wrong, Pat.'

Kennedy took a deep breath and sniffed.

'What you want today?' he asked. 'Pancakes.'

'Just coffee, thanks.'

'Sure, son. Lemme know when you need a refill.'

Their conversations were mostly like that; the way men talk with each other in the absence of women. The least possible amount of words to convey maximum information

The tourist family behind Early talked as they read the menu. He zoned them out and scanned the wall in front of him. On Friday nights, Kennedy's diner was where all the high school kids used to hang out before the football games. There were faded photographs on the wall of the best and bravest from the school's history. Early Simms was there, kneeling in the sunshine with his helmet on the ground in front of him and smiling broadly in his uniform.

Early and some of his friends used to come in after practice too. He remembered one such day when he was seventeen; seeing the girl with dark hair and long legs. It seemed like it had been more than eighteen years ago.

The kids didn't come so much now, no matter what time of day. Just old geezers like Shurmur. The football program at the school closed for good a few years ago – a result of dwindling student numbers. The area had increasingly become a place where more and more homes lay empty during the winter months – used only for vacationers during summer time. It wasn't like 1988 when they won the state championship and one of the linemen was drafted to the NFL. Or later when everyone thought that Early might become the best linebacker that had ever played the game.

Shurmur saw Early staring at the photographs.

'You were the best I ever seen,' he told Early. 'That's the truth.'

Early looked at Shurmur for a long moment. Shurmur could not hold his gaze and turned back to his coffee. Early took a five-dollar bill from his wallet, put it on the counter and left, the bell sounding behind him as he closed the door.

'What I say?' Shurmur asked.

Pat Kennedy watched Early striding across the street towards the sheriff's office.

'Wasn't anything you said, old man,' he told Shurmur. 'Kid had a bad day is all.'

Shurmur rubbed at a faded tattoo on his forearm. It brought back memories of young men in a jungle far away; a country that none of them had ever heard of before.

'He better get ready for plenty more to come,' he said.

3

Blackwater was like most small towns on Cape Cod – busy with tourists in the summer months and empty during the winter. Early liked the winter best, when the temperature was more comfortable and the place felt like it belonged to the locals instead of the weekenders from Boston and beyond.

The town sat at the southern edge of the Cape, a few miles from Woods Hole which was located on Buzzards Bay. It was a short hop from there to the Elizabeth Islands and then into Rhode Island Sound.

There were public beaches in Blackwater down on Oyster Road and, further west, private beaches for a couple of hotels and some of the bigger, beach-front residences. Mostly they were summer houses for city dwellers.

The town itself did not amount to much. Highway 28 from mainland Massachusetts became Reunion Highway from which you could continue west towards Woods Hole or turn east onto Main Street. It was Early's experience that almost every town on the island had a 'Main Street'. It made navigation simple. If you got lost, you stopped and asked a local where 'Main' was.

From Main Street you could head south to the beaches along Oyster Road, east to the shopping mall on Grand Straits, further east again onto Blackwater Highway towards Mashpee and Hyannis or north to one of the two streets that ran parallel to Main: Elm Road and then Briar Street.

The high school where Early had played football was off Elm Road, with the small stadium– now no more than rotting wooden bleachers and a field full of weeds – across the street. Early's girlfriend back then had been Kate Foley – a quiet girl prone to reading books and wearing denim shorts in summer. Funny the things you remember. Most of Early's buddies gravitated towards the cheerleaders but that wasn't Early's thing. Not that she wasn't pretty, just not as obvious as some.

They broke up after what happened. Early retreated into himself – became distant and sullen. Now, the doctors would diagnose depression or post-traumatic stress disorder and prescribe him a course of happy pills. But that wasn't what you did as an eighteen-year-old tough guy. You rode it out on your own.

Kate left for Boston College after they graduated at the end of that year. She came to see Early the day she left, though they had not been together for some months. She stood in the doorway of his home, her hands hidden inside the sleeves of a too-big sweatshirt with the college name printed on it. She wore plain white sneakers and pale blue shorts. Her dark hair was tied up except for the loose strands that fell around her face. He couldn't remember her ever looking so beautiful.

They had a short conversation. He was uncommunicative and couldn't look at her for very long without feeling a knot squeezing his intestines.

Then she left.

He'd seen her a few times since then, but not for a while. Her parents still lived in one of the few big beach houses owned by a local along Oyster Road, past Quisset Sands. He heard from Shirley Lee, the sheriff's department secretary and gossip, that Kate had followed her father's career path and was a criminal lawyer now in Boston. She visited with her parents every summer and was married to a guy that ran a restaurant somewhere in the city.

The last time Early saw her was three summers ago. She

was walking along Main Street on her own one Tuesday morning and passed by Kennedy's Diner as Early ate his breakfast. That was when his dad still recognised him and he was feeling good that day. She had not aged much that he could tell. She walked by without looking into the diner.

'Say, isn't that the girl you used to date?' Pat Kennedy had said when he saw who Early was looking at.

'Don't know,' Early told him, forking eggs into his mouth.

'Sure it is. What's her name, now?'

Early did not answer.

Early walked across the street from Kennedy's and up two steps into the sheriff's office. Shirley Lee sat behind a counter facing the door. She was banging away on an old typewriter, refusing to acknowledge the computer that sat unused behind her. An electric fan was whirring on the counter, working hard against the heat.

Shirley's grey hair was cut short – 'dyke short' was how she described it – and she was wearing her standard summer uniform: a white cotton skirt with a green linen blouse. She liked to wear green because it matched the shirts that the sheriff and his deputies wore. Made her feel more official.

Early grabbed the handle of a door to the right of the counter.

'Mornin,' Shirley,' he said.

She stopped thumping the keys and looked up at him.

'Hey, Early. How's your dad doing?'

'Same as before. Can you buzz me through?'

She knew better than to probe and pressed a button under the counter to open the secure door to the inner office.

Early went through the door and along a short hallway that ended at the sheriff's office. On the right, facing onto Main Street, was a large room that Early shared with the other two deputies: Randolph Jones and Frank Wood. Both men were at their desks, talking about the Red Sox game from the previous night. Early stopped at the open door and said hello before moving on towards the sheriff's room.

On his left Early passed what they called the kitchen, though it was no more than a cupboard they had converted to house a small refrigerator and a coffee machine. The restroom, which they all shared, was the last door on the left.

There were no prisoner holding facilities in the building. This was down to a combination of size and the lack of any serious crime. Anyone that needed time in a cell before court was transported to the nearest pre-arraignment detention facility at Barnstable County Jail on the southern edge of the Camp Edwards military training base.

Early rapped on the sheriff's door and went in. The office was nearly as large as the room the three deputies shared and was on the corner of the building with windows on both walls. Light streamed in through open blinds. Sheriff Henry Kapnick – 'Kappy' to those that knew him well – had the phone to his ear and held up a single finger to tell Early to wait. Early stepped into the room and closed the door.

On the wall behind the door was the department's armoury: a set of double doors concealing a rack containing two pump-action shotguns, spare handguns for each member of the department, boxes of bullets and shotgun shells and ballistic vests that none of them had ever had the occasion to wear.

Early walked to the desk and sat in one of the chairs across from Kapnick. The sheriff was ten years older than Early and had been in his post since Charlie Simms retired. Early still remembered Kapnick from his school days when Kapnick was a raw deputy. He had enjoyed rousting under-age members of the football team on a Saturday night for drinking beer down on the beach. So far as Early could tell, the man had not mellowed. He still had a mean streak that surfaced from time to time, most notably earlier in the year when he subdued a motorist who had, Kapnick claimed, resisted attempts to arrest him on a DUI charge. The motorist got a broken nose and fractured thumb for his troubles. Not to mention a three-month jolt at Barnstable County Jail for resisting. The man now in jail was Manu Polite, a local bruiser known for being able to handle himself.

Kapnick came from fisherman stock, with thick forearms and wide shoulders. He was cultivating a bit of a gut as well, his leather belt creaking when he put the phone down and leaned forward. He had a big head, with sparse hair cut short and a thick salt and pepper moustache.

'You up for a trip to Bourne today?' Kapnick asked.

Early shrugged and said sure.

'Want to know what it's about, first?'

'I'll enjoy the drive.'

Kapnick leaned back in his chair, a shaft of sunlight cutting across his body.

'Your dad not so good today?'

Early was tired of answering the same question. He looked out the window and saw the English tourists exit the diner across the street. The father lifted the girl into his arms and kissed her on the cheek. She laughed and wrapped her arms around his neck.

Early turned back to Kapnick.

'What's the job?'

4

What would the pilgrims think of out of town shopping centres, Kate Foley thought as she turned off Route 3 towards Colony Place and its 'more than forty shops and restaurants'. The main body of Plymouth town disappeared in her rear-view mirror as she drove west towards the 'largest outdoor shopping centre in the region'. The signs advertising Colony Place were not subtle.

Kate pulled into a gas station at the entrance to the shopping centre, taking a wide-brimmed straw hat from the passenger seat of her car and putting it on with sunglasses before getting out. She swiped a credit card through the pump and started filling the tank, catching sight of her reflection in the car window and seeing the trace of bruising around her left eye that extended beyond the reach of her glasses. A man in a suit got out of a Mercedes sedan at the next pump and she angled her head so that he could not see her face.

The car parking spaces nearest the shops were busiest. When the car's tank was full Kate drove to the farthest extreme of the parking lot and looked for a spot facing away from the shops and as far from any other cars as she could manage. She felt the spasms start before the car came to a stop and pressed her foot hard on the brake, bringing the car to a sudden halt. Pulling the keys from the ignition, she covered her face with her hands and let the tears come freely, the sobs convulsing her body.

John Lustig, Kate's husband of three years, had seemed like the perfect date after a lot of years and as many men. He owned a restaurant where he used to be the head chef. He was attentive, could cook and wasn't averse to cleaning up after himself. The jealous streak he had managed to keep hidden until six months ago when he started rifling through her bag, checking her e-mails and obsessing over the call records for her cell phone.

They had some blazing arguments over his behaviour but none had ever amounted to anything except maybe an over-firm grip on her arm when he was making a point. Until last night.

Kate took a tissue from her bag and dabbed at her face. She pulled down the sun visor and flipped open the mirror, taking the first good look at the damage since she had run from the house, blood staining the front of her t-shirt.

Her left eye was swollen half-shut and a ragged gash cut through her eyebrow. It was still moist and the tissue came away red when she pressed it to the wound.

'Gonna leave a mark,' she told herself.

She pressed a hand to her side and winced at the pain from her bruised ribs. John had caught her with at least two good body shots.

Her hair was a mess. It was naturally curly and she wore it to her shoulders. But blood, tears and five hours sleep in the car at a rest stop had matted it badly. She felt like crap and in need of a shower. She made do for now tying her hair back with a scrunchy and taking a few deep breaths to settle herself.

She still didn't know what she was going to do; had not been to a hospital or the police. The car had almost auto-piloted south from Boston towards her parents' house in Blackwater before she saw the signs for this place and noticed that the petrol gauge was not far off empty. Now she wasn't so sure she wanted her dad to see her like this. He was a man of infinite patience, except when it came to the wellbeing of his only daughter. The last thing she wanted was a confrontation between him and John.

It was funny how a smart, successful professional could fall apart so easily after a good beating.

5

It was a short drive north on Highway 28 from Blackwater to the Barnstable County Correctional Facility near Bourne. Early was on the road after ten and drove with the windows up and the air on full. Frank Wood sat beside Early wearing aviator sunglasses and resting one shiny boot on the dashboard in front of him.

'Take your foot off my car, please, Frank.'

Wood was the youngest of the three deputies at twenty-five and still going through a phase of thinking he was the toughest guy you could ever meet. Early knew what that was like. Putting on the dark green shirt emblazoned with the badge of office and buckling up the belt weighed down with a handgun, radio receiver, handcuffs and pepper spray made you feel invincible for a while. But it passed quickly for Early – became a job like any other.

Frank Wood, Early could tell, still thought it was cool.

Wood slowly lowered his foot onto the floor, pinching the crease of his beige pants when he was done, making sure they were still sharp.

Wood was like a lot of the younger cops that Early met now: tight shirts bulging with gym manufactured muscles and no clue how to manage a heated situation without resorting to the threat of violence. Or actual violence.

Early's teammates from high school would have been confused by their former friend's apparently placid nature. Thing was, back then Early Simms could kick anyone's ass and not even break a sweat doing it. He was a man who relished physical violence, whether on the football field or off of it. And he was good at it. So there was no need for bravado or show. If things got hot on a Saturday night, Early was the one man on the team they knew they could rely on to have their back. He never raised his voice or made threats. If you picked on him or a buddy of his, he would go off on you without hesitation or warning.

'So, what's the story on this thing?' Wood asked. 'I mean, why all the secrecy?'

'If I knew that, it wouldn't be a secret.'

'You're a funny guy, Early.'

'People have said that.'

Wood snorted.

'Come on,' Wood said. 'I don't believe the sheriff dint tell you anything.'

That was another thing about Wood; the way he talked. He said things like 'dint' instead of 'didn't' and 'coont' instead of 'couldn't'.

Early sighed. He knew he would not get any peace on the journey unless he told Wood what was going on.

'You remember the guy that the sheriff put down after he resisted?'

'Manu Polite? Isn't he due for release this week?'

'Tomorrow,' Early nodded

'What about him?' Wood asked.

'Seems somebody took a serious dislike to him last night.'

'No shit. What happened?'

'Jailhouse shank made out of a sharpened toothbrush. Some guy stabbed him in the neck and back.'

Wood pushed his department baseball cap back on his head and gave a low whistle.

'Think Kappy put some con up to it?' Wood asked, winking at Early and jabbing his right hand forward, stabbing at an imaginary foe.

Early didn't think it was such a bad guess, though he knew Wood was joking. Sheriff Kapnick had not gained his reputation by accident.

'I doubt it,' he told Wood. 'And it's Sheriff Kapnick to you.'

Wood half-turned to Early and held up both hands.

'Sorry, boss.'

'Sheriff just wants it handled…sensitively, you know.'

'Early Simms is your man for sensitivity, is that it?' Wood said, putting his boot back on the dashboard.

Early turned his head and stared at Wood, keeping the car straight on the road and maintaining a steady sixty miles an hour. The grin on Wood's face faltered.

'Foot,' Early said.

Wood dropped his boot to the floor.

'Don't make me have to tell you again.'

6

They drove past Megansett Harbor and Cataumet to the west before turning east through the woods along Connery Avenue. From there, Early drove onto Sheriff's Plaza which opened to the tarmac parking lot in front of the main jail building. The new Correctional Facility had been built in 2004 and sat on a square plot of land surrounded by trees on all sides. It was within the Edwards military reservation but not subject to the rigid security perimeter and regulations.

The jail buildings were no higher than two storeys at any one point. Early parked the car close to the main entrance and walked briskly to the doors with Wood almost skipping to keep up with the bigger man's long strides.

Once inside, they stopped at a security desk with a sign on the wall that read 'No Weapons Beyond This Point' and handed over their weapons. The duty officer locked them in a safe behind his desk. From there, another officer took them through a red, metal door into a wide corridor that led to a green door with 'House 2' printed on it – one of the units housing the male prisoners. The place reminded Early of a hospital, with pale floors and walls that smelled of cleaning fluid and bleach. The plain floor was broken up at irregular intervals by dark green or red tiles.

The officer with them was a black man, almost as tall as Early but without his wide shoulders and thick arms. The man had a moustache. Not for the first time Early wondered what it was about being a police or a correctional officer that inclined men to grow moustaches.

'Guy that did it is in there,' the officer said, pointing to another door, this one with 'Pod F' painted above it.

Early knew that 'the Pod' was for difficult prisoners who were kept separate from the general population and locked down in the cells for twenty-three out of every twenty-four hours.

'You want to speak to him after we been to medical services?'

Early said maybe and followed the officer past the entrance to the Pod and along another wide corridor. They passed the library and entered the medical services unit through a secure door. The officer banged it shut behind them.

'Second bed on the right,' he said, pointing with his chin. 'You know he don't want to press charges, right? What he told me.'

Early said he knew.

The room was big enough for three beds on each side. The walls and floor were in the same pale, institutional tones as the corridors and above the smell of bleach were faint hints of blood and vomit. There were small windows with interior bars high on the walls allowing the sun to brighten the place. It was a relief to be away from the faint buzz of strip lights that illuminated the rest of the facility. Only one other bed was occupied. The man in it was snoring loud enough to rattle the plastic cup on the table beside his bed.

There was another corrections officer sitting at a desk on the far wall. He wore the regulation navy blue uniform with the facility's badge and a silver nametag. He looked up at Early and nodded.

Wood followed Early to the bed occupied by the man they were here to see. Manu Polite was lying on his side facing away from the entrance. He had turned his head when Early came into the room and was doing his best to appear nonchalant.

Early had little doubt that Kapnick assaulted Polite

without justification. He'd seen enough of his boss to know what the man was capable of. He also knew that Manu Polite was not a man to garner much sympathy. Polite was forty-one and had been convicted of numerous assaults and minor drug charges. He was of Samoan descent, with short, dark hair and a rich, brown tone to his skin. He wasn't tall, less than six feet, but built like a pick-up truck. Early guessed that Kapnick had put cuffs on Polite before taking to him with his baton. Otherwise, Polite would have been a pretty good match for the sheriff.

Early stopped beside Polite's bed with Wood behind him. Early saw a dressing on the Samoan's neck spotted with blood. It didn't look like his assailant had done too much damage.

'How are you doing, Manu?' Early asked.

Polite turned his big head and stared at Early. Early grinned.

'Fuck you,' Polite said.

'Come on, man,' Early said, hooking his thumbs in his belt. 'Don't be like that. I asked a civil question.'

'You can tell the sheriff that he doesn't need to send his dogs to check on me. Anyway, I already said that I don't want to make anything of this.'

'You're a hard case, Manu. Is that it?'

Early was goading him deliberately, knowing that Polite had a short fuse.

Polite turned quickly, throwing his bed clothes half off his body. Early did not react. The officer that had brought Early and Frank Wood to the room told Polite to settle down of he'd end up in the Pod. Polite glared at the man but said nothing. He had no desire to be locked in a cell alone for most of the day.

'I'm tough enough,' Polite told Early.

'I'm investigating an assault. It's my job,'

'I told you I didn't make no complaint.'

'You know that anything in here has to be reported, Manu. But are you saying you don't want to press charges?'

'That's right.'

Early tilted his head to one side.

'Don't go thinking you can settle this on your own terms,' he told Polite. 'I mean, you're due out tomorrow. Don't want to be in here any longer than you have to be.'

Polite reached over his shoulder and rubbed at the dressing on his neck.

'Ain't nothin' but a scratch.'

Early made a show of looking around the room.

'So why you need to be in here?'

Polite dropped his hands onto his lap and shrugged.

'I didn't ask to be.'

'Policy, huh?'

Polite shrugged again.

'Okay,' Early said. 'You take it easy now, you hear? Don't go busting anyone's head.'

'What do you care?'

'I'm a peace officer.'

Polite grunted a laugh and grabbed at his crotch.

'Piece of this,' he said.

'Now, that's just plain rude,' Early told him, turning to leave.

Early went out to the parking lot after collecting his weapon and leaned against the car while Wood went to the rest room inside the facility. It was hotter still, though a bank of cloud looked to be heading for the island from the south. Early though that a little summer rain would be just fine. He felt the heat of the sun drawn in through the dark material of his shirt and drew an arm across his forehead, wiping away a thin layer of sweat.

His cell phone buzzed on his belt. He took it from its holder and saw that it was the number of the department's main switchboard. He heard Shirley Lee's voice when he answered.

'Sheriff says he wants you to take a call, Early,' she said. 'You finished at the jail?'

'Yeah, what's up?'

'Got a domestic violence call.'

'How bad?'

'Not sure. Woman got beat on by her husband. Her father called it in.'

'What's the address?'

'Twenty-one seventeen Oyster.'

Early frowned. Shirley must have gotten the wrong address.

'Say again?'

She repeated the same number.

'You sure that's right?'

'Yeah, uh huh. Why, something wrong?'

Early said that it was fine and he would take the call. He hung up on Shirley and put his phone away. Frank Wood pushed open the main door of the jail and walked towards Early.

'Got a call, Frank,' Early shouted. 'I'm going to drop you back at the station and take it myself.'

Wood jogged to the car and said that was fine with him.

Early knew the house where the complaint had originated. It belonged to Bree and Joe Foley – Kate's parents.

7

'I don't know the name of this place,' Marshall Cain said to his younger brother, Jimmy. 'What is it?'

They were in a bar somewhere south of Boston. Jimmy didn't know the name of the town or the bar and told Marshall as much. It got to the stage sometimes that Jimmy identified these towns only by the number of bars on the main street.

'Some two-bar shit hole,' he said.

Marshall laughed. He still found it funny no matter how many times he heard it.

'I need to go,' Marshall said.

Jimmy said whatever and took a long drink of the beer sitting on the bar in front of him. His brother walked to the end of the counter and turned to his left heading towards the restroom. He passed a group of four men playing pool and drinking bourbon. Marshall was shorter than Jimmy at five-eight and built solidly. He wore jeans, a black t-shirt under a denim shirt and a faded Patriots baseball cap.

'Eight ball, top left,' Marshall said to the man leaning down to take his turn at the table, lightly nudging the end of the pool cue the man was holding.

Marshall didn't stop or see the glare from the man. Jimmy watched the group after Marshall had disappeared into the restroom. The man that had been about to take the shot stood and said something quietly to his friends. He was short and broad with a wide backside. His friends looked like they came off a conveyer belt for twitchy, wiry types distinguished only by their haircuts: long, shaved and spiked.

Spike looked at Jimmy and smirked.

Jimmy took another pull on his beer and held the man's gaze until he looked away.

Jimmy was twenty-seven, five foot eleven with short brown hair and a lithely athletic build. The only thing he had enjoyed in school was baseball, at which he excelled. He trained hard in the gym and played tough. After leaving school, he found work as a car mechanic and the physical nature of the work kept him in decent shape. He augmented it by working out at the local boxing gym where he worked the heavy bag and sparred with some of the younger guys. He took it easy on them, mostly.

Jimmy knew about anger. He was aware of his own capacity for violence. He thought of it in the way a mechanic would – as if a wire had been soldered in the wrong place in his brain. Someone had once described Marshall to Jimmy as 'half Scots, half scumbag', a reference to his parents' Celtic heritage: his dad a Scotsman; and his mother one generation removed from Ireland.

Jimmy put the guy in the hospital, nearly in the ground.

He served eighteen months for it. Got off light. Turned out the guy was carrying a knife in his back pocket which garnered some sympathy from the DA that agreed the plea deal with Jimmy's lawyer.

William James Cain, Jimmy and Marshall's father, had spent eight years married to their mother without spending much time at home. Mostly he was out screwing around. Even at a young age Jimmy had an idea about why his mother cried herself to sleep most nights alone in her bed. Big Billy Cain left one morning and never returned.

Jimmy remembered his father as a permanently angry man, a frown always creasing his brow. He was prone to long periods of silence – a psychological form of abuse that seemed to hurt his mother more than any physical pain that could have been inflicted. Beyond that, Jimmy had no recollection of the man; couldn't really even picture him in his head after more than twenty years. Maybe he inherited his anger from Big Billy.

Their mother spent the rest of her life – which ended two days ago at age fifty-nine – in a fog of depression and prescription medication. This road trip was kind of an extended wake for her. Jimmy had a picture of her in his wallet. It was one half of her wedding photo, torn down the middle, erasing Big Billy from her history. Jimmy found it after the funeral. She looked kind of pretty. He had never thought of her in that way before.

Jimmy was two years younger than Marshall, but had spent most of his life looking after his brother. When their mother drank, which was often after her husband left, she was prone to lashing out. The boys soon learned to keep out of her way.

What came to be known as 'Marshall's accident' happened on a Saturday night when rain and wind battered their apartment building. The boys knew well enough to stay in their room when their mother worked up a head of steam with a bottle of vodka, but that night she had descended to some deeper level of personal hell and her screaming sobs were too much for Marshall.

Jimmy pulled a pillow over his head and pressed it to his ears to drown out the noise. Marshall, tears streaming down his face bolted from his bed beside Jimmy and ran to his mother. Jimmy tried to stop him. He had a vivid image in his head of his fingertips brushing his brother's jammies as older boy ran. He often wondered how different things might have been if he'd caught Marshall and what happened next had never been.

But it had.

Jimmy got to his mother's bedroom in time to see Marshall's feet go out from under him as his mother's hand crashed onto the side of his head. Marshall went down, his head cracking off the iron bedpost. He landed in a limp heap on the bare floor. Jimmy ran to his brother, fear and rage welling inside him. Blood smeared the floor and Jimmy's hands as he cradled his brother's head in his lap. His mother lay on the bed breathing in shallow gasps, her hands covering her face.

Marshall had been a spirited child before that night. He changed irreversibly after it; became reckless and seemingly unaware of danger in the things that he did. And a few years ago Jimmy caught him kissing a thirteen-year-old girl outside of their apartment building one night. The girl looked older than she was and played it tough when Jimmy told her to go home. Marshall claimed that she told him that she was eighteen, but she had not looked that old and it was an incident that Jimmy had not forgotten

Spike kept shooting glances at Jimmy while the others in his group got back to playing pool. The big guy stared at the restroom door when he wasn't at the table taking a shot.

Jimmy knew that the men at the pool table were getting ready to lay it hard and heavy on Marshall when he came back into the main part of the bar. That was going be a real bad idea for all of them. Marshall couldn't take four all on his own, though he would try, but Jimmy was pretty sure that the two of them together would have no problem. People often underestimated their ability to inflict pain because they didn't look like much at first.

The bar was bright, sunlight coming in through two big windows either side of the entrance. It smelled of spilled beer and old cigarette smoke. A lone, old drunk was half-slumped on a table by the door nursing a nearly empty whisky. Other than him and the four would-be tough guys playing pool the only other person was the bartender who was watching ESPN on the TV fixed above the bar.

Jimmy looked at the spare pool cue in the rack this side of the pool table and sat forward on the edge of his barstool. He pushed his shoulders back and rubbed his hands on his jeans.

8

Marshall came out of the restroom and the four men made their first mistake, all of them turning at the sound of the door.

Jimmy got up, fast and light on his feet. Marshall saw his brother moving in a blur before he was aware of the four men and their intentions. He knew what his brother's move meant.

Jimmy shouted 'hey' loudly as he reached the corner of the bar counter, grabbing the spare pool cue from the rack.

Second mistake: they looked away from Marshall at the shout.

That was the idea.

Marshall grabbed a ball from the table and threw it at Shaved. It hit him on the side of the head, sending him to the floor.

Jimmy swung the pool cue into the wide guy's face, splintering both the wood and several of the man's teeth. Blood sprayed the front of the guy's shirt and he dropped to the floor as well, rolling onto his stomach and mewling like a cat. His shirt rode up on his back exposing a revolver tucked into the waistband of his jeans.

Spike looked at Long, neither of them prepared for this. Long dropped his cue onto the pool table and backed away from Marshall as he advanced on him. Long held his hands up and shook his head.

Spike looked at Jimmy and reached one hand behind his

back.

Jimmy knew he was going for a gun.

Marshall grabbed Long's cue from the table and hit Spike high on his forehead, laying open a seven-inch gash and knocking him onto a table where he lay still and bleeding. A handgun dropped onto the floor beside him.

Long backed into the corner of the bar and looked ready to puke.

The wide guy continued to squeal on the floor.

Jimmy nodded at Marshall. They took a gun each and backed away from the carnage they had wrought.

The bartender stared at Jimmy.

'They started it, man,' Jimmy said.

'Sure, whatever,' the bartender replied.

Marshall whooped and wiped a sleeve across his face, smearing someone's blood like war paint.

Jimmy grabbed his brother's arm and pulled him out the door into the sunlight.

9

The Foley house on Oyster Road was classic Cape Cod. It had a big front yard facing the road and a porch at the back for enjoying the sunset. The wood was painted pale blue with a grey shingle roof. It had five bedrooms and three bathrooms over three floors. A narrow path snaked through the back yard, stopping at a short fence that led directly onto a private part of the beach shared with the two houses on either side. It was, Kate Foley had always thought, idyllic.

'You okay in there, honey?' Kate's mother, Bree, called from outside the bathroom on the first-floor hall.

Kate Foley told her mother that she was fine, raising her voice to be heard through the closed door. She turned back to the mirror and pressed a finger gingerly to the cut above her eye.

'You look like shit,' she told herself, a thin smile starting on her lips.

She could hear the silence of her mother hovering outside; heard the quiet creak of floorboards as she strained to hear what her daughter was doing.

'I'll be down in a minute, Mom, so go put the coffee on.'

More creaking.

'Please, Mom.'

'Don't be too long.'

Kate got her make-up bag and did her best to obscure the bruising on her face. It was better than nothing. Outside, a large capacity car engine rumbled as the vehicle came to a slow stop on the front driveway. Someone got out and walked to the door. Sounded like it was a large man from the noise his fist made on the wooden door.

She pushed the bathroom window open, the salt smell of the sea flooding into the room on a light breeze. Her father had answered the door and she could hear him speaking to the man from the car as they moved into the hallway. She looked out the open window and saw a sheriff's department patrol car in the driveway.

'Damn it, dad,' she hissed.

Kate heard voices in the living room that faced the rear of the property. She turned at the bottom of the stairs and went through the double doors into the room, her eyes sweeping across the view of the ocean outside the window. She stopped when she saw Early Simms stand up from the couch where he had been sitting with her father.

Early had a cap in his hands which he twisted as he stood, the skin of his knuckles stretching to white.

'Hey, Kate,' he said.

Oh, Jesus, don't cry, she thought. *Not in front of him.*

She felt tears close to the surface; lifted a hand to her mouth and bit hard at the skin of her index finger. The pain cleared her head, held back the tears.

'Early,' she nodded, her voice wavering a little. 'How are you? It's been a while.'

She glared at her father who was still on the couch. He was unmoved. He mother stood next to her father at the far end of the couch. She was a woman that always held herself erect. Her hair was dyed blonde to cover the fact that it was now mostly grey and cut short and neat. Kate always remembered her as being smartly presented. She had not worked after Kate was born.

'I'm fine,' Early said. 'Looks like you can't say the same. I mean, that's a real shiner you've got there.'

He had aged well, was what she thought. Still had those big shoulders and wide chest pressing against the cloth of his shirt. His biceps flexed as he twisted the cap. He looked good in uniform.

'It was an accident, you know. And, anyway, I'd rather not talk about it.'

She stared at her father again.

'I thought I had made that clear already.'

Early looked at her father and back at Kate. She felt less assured under his gaze, wanting to tell him what had happened and see him do something about it. She knew that he could.

'Why don't you sit down, Kate, and we can talk about it. I mean, what happened to your face. If you don't want to take it any further – you know, press charges or whatever – we can leave it at that. It's up to you.'

She knew that cop tone of voice; had heard it a hundred times in her job. It was equal parts comforting and patronising, soothing and threatening. But she could feel it working on her.

Or maybe it was just him. Her feeling vulnerable after what had happened and being close to him again after all this time.

'I think that's a good idea, honey,' her mom said.

Kate did not look at her mom. She did not know what to say to Early. She crossed her arms over her chest, regretting how defensive it would make her look but holding the pose nonetheless.

'You want me to go?' Early asked.

Kate walked to a worn leather chair with a straight back – what her dad called his thinking chair – and sat in it, curling her legs up under her. The room was decorated in pastels, with a dark wood floor.

Early looked at her parents.

'Joe. Bree. Why don't you give me some time to find out what happened,' Early said. 'Let me do my job.'

Joseph Foley looked from Early to his daughter. She inclined her head, which he took for a yes.

'Let me know if you need anything, Early,' Joe said,

shaking Early's hand before turning to follow his wife from the room.

Standing next to Early, Joe had looked like he belonged to a different species. Joe was almost six feet tall with a thick head of white hair, but was much slimmer. Kate thought he looked almost half Early's size.

Early sat on the couch and put his cap on the floor between his feet. He pointed at her face.

'Has that happened before?'

'What did my dad tell you?'

Early leaned back into the couch and rubbed at his jaw.

'Said you showed up here in a bad way. That your husband hit you.'

Kate chewed at a thumbnail and turned to look out at the ocean.

'Is that true?' Early asked. 'I mean, that he hit you?'

She felt the tears coming again and this time couldn't hold them back completely. She sniffed and wiped at her eyes with the heel of a hand.

'Did you know that I was a lawyer?' she asked.

Early said that he did.

'Criminal law,' she added. 'I've represented some pretty bad guys, you know. Been in holding areas in police stations and in major prisons. Much worse than anything you have here, Deputy Simms.'

She smiled for the first time.

'You're a tough guy now, Kate. Is that it?' Early asked, returning her smile.

'Yeah, can't you tell from my face?'

'You should see the other guy, right?'

Kate laughed. She felt comfortable in this man's presence. Perhaps more so than with any other man she'd met. And that included her father. There was a calm about him that had not been present when they were together all those years ago.

'What I mean,' Kate said, 'is that I've been around violent men all my working life. And I never even saw it coming. It's so…'

She trailed off, going back to chewing at her nail.

'You feel angry,' Early said.

'I feel ashamed.'

Early shifted on the couch, the leather of his belt and holster creaking. A door opened somewhere in the house and that sweet sea air drifted into the room. A gull called out overhead.

'If you want to report an assault you need to do it back where it happened,' Early told her. 'In Boston.'

'I don't know why my dad called you.'

'Well, he didn't exactly call *me*.'

'You know what I mean.'

'I expect he was worried about you. Maybe he wanted to protect you. Or, at least, feel like he was protecting you. Dads are like that.'

She said maybe; asked him how his dad was. He swallowed hard before answering.

'He's not so good. Alzheimer's.'

Kate sat forward.

'Oh, Early. I'm sorry. I always liked your dad.'

'He liked you too.'

She stood with her back to him and looked out of the window. She could hear him breathing. A yacht drifted on the ocean.

Early came off the couch and stood beside her. He slipped his cap on and put his hands in his pockets.

'It's beautiful here,' he said.

'Sometimes I wonder why I didn't come back after college.'

'What answer do you come up with?'

'I don't have one. Not really.'

She turned to face him, looking up and remembering what it used to be like to be enveloped by those big arms of his. She was struck by a memory so strong: of pressing her face against his chest after *that* football game and smelling soap and tears on his skin. He was never the same after that.

'You look older,' she said, putting the tip of her finger against the crow's feet developing at his eyes.

He didn't move to stop her. She felt self-conscious and dropped her hand.

'We all got older,' he said.

10

John Lustig, Kate Foley's husband, sat in the living room of the Boston apartment he shared with his wife and flexed the fingers of his right hand. It felt stiff and sore and the first two knuckles were crusted with lines of blood from the scratches in his skin. He rubbed his other hand over the knuckles as if that would soothe the pain.

The room was semi-dark with the blinds closed and the curtains pulled shut. He had switched the air off and was starting to sweat as the room grew warmer. His cell phone wriggled on the table beside the chair, vibrating as another call got missed. He'd lost count after the first ten. Mostly they were from his restaurant. He couldn't face it today.

He was trying to remember how it got so out of hand with Kate last night but it was like trying to grasp clouds. His mind was fuzzy, as if half of it was made of cotton wool. He'd felt like that for a while now.

Am I going crazy? he wondered. *Is this what mental illness feels like?*

Kate had been shouting about something was what he thought about last night. He had gotten home first. Maybe he'd been looking through her stuff again. He had to do that. She needed to be watched. She was up to something. Maybe fucking that new lawyer at her office.

Lustig frowned and pressed his fingers to the space between his eyes.

He smelled something then. He wasn't sure what. A noise

formed in his head: hissing and crackling. He coughed, his throat dry and scratchy, and noticed that his vision was blurred.

He got up and walked to the hall. The smell was worse there and the air thick. He walked to the end of the hall and through the last door into the kitchen. Two pieces of what used to be bacon lay in a frying pan belching smoke. They were black and sticking to the pan.

Lustig grabbed a cloth, soaked it in water and held it over his mouth and nose. His eyes watered and he coughed hard.

He looked at the ceiling and saw that the smoke alarm had been smashed. Pieces of the plastic covering crunched under his feet as he went to the cooker and grabbed the frying pan. He threw it in the sink, turned the cold water on and went into the hall, bending over to draw in some less polluted air.

He went back to the living room and sat in the same seat, dropping the wet cloth on the floor. He looked down at his injured hand and rubbed at the scratched knuckles. He tried to remember what he'd been doing in the kitchen but could not.

Something hard pressed uncomfortable into the small of his back. He reached back and grasped a handgun. He stared at the gun for a while.

Then stared at it some more.

11

Early drove to the sheriff's office from the Foley house by a roundabout route. That son of a bitch husband had really gone after her, he thought. Back in the day he'd have been out looking for the man. Not now.

He knew some cops up in Boston. You got to meet like-minded individuals in the law enforcement community. You never knew when you might need a favour. He thought about calling someone. Have them visit Kate's husband. Just say: hi, how are ya?

But that wasn't what she wanted. Not yet anyway. Early had made the offer before he left the house and she had declined.

'Maybe later,' were her exact words.

Early didn't want to do anything that would hurt her. He reckoned he'd done enough of that when he was a younger man. She needed to find her own resolution and he'd help if that's what she wanted.

The cloudbank that had threatened to spoil the hot summer day had made good on its early promise. The sun was obscured as Early parked by the office. It didn't look like it would rain, but the temperature had dropped by a good five degrees and a light wind ambled up the main street when he got out of the car.

Early went to Sheriff Kapnick's office and found his boss standing by one of the windows drinking coffee from a Red Sox mug.

'You knew that call related to Kate Foley' Early said.

Kapnick did not turn around.

'You help her out?' he asked.

Early shrugged, more to himself than Kapnick.

'It happened in the city. She'll have to decide if she wants to help herself.'

Kapnick took a drink from his mug and walked to his desk without looking directly at Early. He put his mug on the desk, sat down and stretched his hands behind his head. Dark circles of sweat showed under his arms.

'You want to know how I got on with Manu Polite?' Early asked.

Kapnick said sure, though Early was certain that the sheriff had already received a call from a friendly corrections officer at the jail.

'He'll be fine. Man has a thick head.'

Kapnick snorted.

'But you knew that already, right?'

'Manu needs to be careful. He'd be better going back to the islands when he gets out.'

'I got more chance of going to the islands than Manu. He'll be around here.'

'Bad for him if he wants to start something. You hear me, Early?'

Early couldn't understand why the sheriff would want to make more trouble for Polite after he had served his time.

'I need to know if I can count on you for back-up,' Kapnick said, folding his arms across chest.

Early looked out the window and across the street at Kennedy's diner.

'If Manu breaks the law, I'll bring him to book.'

Kapnick stared at the side of Early's head until his deputy turned to face him.

'Good enough,' Early said, not intending it as a question.

He nodded at Kapnick and went down the hall to the room he shared with the other deputies.

The wind was stronger on the beach and Kate Foley pulled her cardigan around her body. She heard her father open the gate that led from the back yard of their house onto the beach and waited for him to speak when he stopped behind her. It was her experience that her father liked to assume control.

'You going to do anything about him?' her father asked after a while. 'John, I mean. After what he did to you.'

She knew that he meant well and she loved him deeply.

'Dad…'

He moved forward to stand beside her and put an arm around her waist, kissing the top of her head and pulling her to him.

'I worry about you,' he said.

'I know, Dad.'

'I mean, practising law in the city is different than it is here.'

'I know that too. I've been doing it for a while now.'

They stood quietly for a few minutes, the sun momentarily breaking through a gap in the cloud cover.

'Can I ask you something?' Kate said.

'Of course.'

'You knew Early Simms was a deputy, right?'

'Yes.'

'Did you ask him to come today? I mean, him specifically.'

'No. Why would I do that?'

'I don't know.'

'I never understood that boy when you were with him.'

'What do you mean?'

'I'm not expressing myself correctly. I think what I mean is that I never liked the fact that you were with him. He scared me, you know.'

Kate turned to look at her father. He stared at the ocean as the clouds covered the sun again.

'Scared you how?' she asked.

'I saw him play football, Kate. He was a violent young

man. And he loved it. More so than his teammates. Then that other boy got killed.'

Kate pulled away from her father.

'That's not fair, Dad. It wasn't his fault.'

He held his hands open at his sides.

'It was his fault, Kate.'

She opened her mouth to protest.

'Don't get me wrong,' her dad said, cutting her off. 'I'm not saying he intended for it to end the way it did. But he meant to hit that boy as hard as he could.'

Kate felt anger rise in her. The wind picked up and pushed her hair across her face.

'That's who he is Kate. Don't mistake the man he's become for anything else.'

Kate pulled stands of hair out of her eyes and squinted at her father.

'I wouldn't look like this if Early had been there,' she said.

'That may be true. But it wouldn't have made make me like him any better.'

12

'You got blood on you,' Jimmy Cain said, pointing at his brother's neck.

Marshall inclined his head as if he'd be able to see it. Jimmy shook his head at his brother's efforts.

'You'll need a mirror, man,' he told Marshall. 'It's on your shirt too. On the collar.'

Marshall pulled his collar out and saw the blood crusted there.

'Why didn't you tell me before now?'

Jimmy shrugged.

'Never noticed it till now.'

'I been walking around like this most of the day.'

'So go wash it off now.'

Marshall stared at his collar some more before releasing it with a huffed breath.

They had driven to a quiet, wooded area after the incident at the bar, drinking a warm six-pack of beer they had picked up the previous day and listening to old rock songs on the radio. Jimmy fell asleep at some point and woke up two hours later. Marshall was still awake, sitting in the silence of the car staring out the windscreen. When Jimmy asked his brother what he was looking at he said 'trees'.

They were sharing an order of fries inside a burger place in Foxboro, not far from Gillette Stadium where the Patriots played their home games. It was close to seven at night and the place was mostly empty. An older man, probably in his early fifties, came in through the door and walked towards the counter. He looked sideways at Marshall and stared at the dried blood on his neck and shirt. Jimmy watched the man order three burgers with fries at the counter. He was tall with thinning hair and dressed in what looked like a modestly priced suit. His tie was pulled loose at his neck: probably ordering for his family after a long day at work. Frown lines creased the skin between his eyes as if he was always unhappy about something.

The man kept looking back at them as he waited for his order.

'You looking at buddy?' Jimmy eventually said to him.

The man turned away from them.

'I said what you looking at?'

Marshall noticed the agitated tone of his brother's voice and looked up. A young woman, no more than eighteen, glanced nervously at Jimmy as she brought the man's order to the counter in a brown paper bag.

'He's got something on his shirt,' the man said, grabbing the bag and turning to head for the door.

'What's it to you?' Marshall asked.

The man walked to the door and pulled it open. He stopped before leaving.

'You want to look like a bum it's up to you.'

He left with the glass door swinging shut behind him. The woman behind the counter turned her back on Jimmy and Marshall, pretending to check the soft drinks dispenser.

Marshall looked at Jimmy.

'You had enough fun yet today big brother?' Jimmy asked

He thought that it might be okay to mess with the guy a little.

'Let's go,' Marshall said, stuffing the last few fries into his mouth and walking fast to the door.

They followed the guy as he drove two miles south of the burger place and pulled into the narrow driveway of a two-story red brick house in what looked like a solidly blue-collar neighbourhood. Neither Jimmy nor Marshall knew the area.

They stopped two doors down from the house and watched the guy get out of his car and walk to the house, pushing open the door and going inside without looking back.

Jimmy said, 'let's go', opened his door and put one foot onto the pavement. He didn't see Marshall take the gun he had picked up in the bar from the glove compartment and put it in the waistband of his jeans, pulling his shirt out and covering the gun.

Marshall jogged to catch up with Jimmy as they walked past the guy's car and towards the front door. Jimmy grabbed the wing mirror and twisted it downwards till it broke. Marshall moved past him towards the door. When he reached it, he didn't stop. He pulled the handle down and stepped right into the house.

Jimmy shouted his brother's name but Marshall wasn't listening. Jimmy smiled, thinking the guy would shit when he saw Marshall walk into his living room.

Jimmy moved towards the door. He heard a woman shout 'get out'.

The door was half open and Jimmy pushed at it, stepping into a short hallway. A door opened on the right into a small living room where Marshall stood inside the door. A thin woman who must have been the guy's wife stood against the far wall. She didn't look happy.

Another door opened at the far end of the hall and the guy in the suit froze when he saw Jimmy. Then he ran at him. Jimmy expected the guy to stop and take a swing at him but instead he dived full length at Jimmy with his face twisted in a snarl. It surprised Jimmy and both men thumped into the wall to the side of the front door and went down in a heap.

Marshall spun around as the guy landed a decent punch on the top of Jimmy's head. He was stronger than he looked and had Jimmy pinned.

Marshall took the gun from his belt and pointed it at the back of the guy's head. He pulled the trigger and shot him dead.

Blood splashed onto Jimmy as the guy crumpled on top of him. The woman in the living room screamed.

Marshall turned and shot her twice in the chest.

13

Jimmy wriggled out from under the dead weight of the man lying on top of him. He tasted the man's blood in his mouth and spat a red blotch onto the floor of the hall. Marshall laughed and covered his mouth with the hand he held the gun in.

'Oh shit,' Marshall said. 'Look at the mess I made.'

He laughed some more.

Jimmy got out from under the man and rubbed at the top of his head where he had been punched. He stood and looked out the front door onto the street. There was no one around so he pushed the door closed and went past Marshall into the living room. The woman was slumped on the floor with her back against the far wall. Blood streaked the wall above her. Her head was bowed with her chin resting on her chest.

Jimmy walked to her body and hunkered down. He lifted her face up and saw her eyes were open, staring at nothing. He let her head drop and put his hand over one of the bullet wounds. It felt warm and blood seeped between his fingers. He wiped his hand on the woman's jeans, a red smear turning purple against the blue fabric.

Jimmy turned to his brother. Marshall was still smirking. For the first time in his life Jimmy wondered if his brother was insane.

'He bought three burgers,' Jimmy said.

Marshall stopped smirking but clearly did not understand what he was being told.

'Someone else is in the house,' Jimmy told him, standing up and walking to the door.

'Must be upstairs,' Marshall said. 'I'll go see.'

He turned to go up the stairs.

'Marshall,' Jimmy said sharply.

His brother stopped and looked at him.

'Don't shoot anyone else. Whoever it is just bring them down here, okay.'

Marshall nodded.

'Tell me that you'll do that,' Jimmy said firmly.

'I won't shoot anyone else.'

Jimmy stood in the doorway leading from the living room into the hall while his brother went up the stairs. He looked down at the body of the man that a few minutes ago had bought burgers and fries for his family after a long day at work. He felt something inside him slip and knew that he would never be the same again after this.

Marshall Cain stood in the hall on the second floor of the house and listened. He held the gun by his side and smelled a cordite tang in the air. There were four rooms off the hall. He figured one would have to be the bathroom and the other three were bedrooms. Whoever was up here probably went into the bathroom because that was usually the only room with a lock. He looked at each door and saw no outward sign of a lock. Must be a sliding bolt on the inside, he thought.

He went to the door at the top of the stairs and pressed his ear against it. After that, he banged the gun against the door, knocking loose some paint and marking the door where he had hit it.

'I'll huff and I'll puff…' he whispered.

Marshall pulled the handle of the door down and pushed. The door did not move.

He stepped back and kicked the door under the handle.

The wood splintered but the door remained closed. He kicked it again and this time the lock broke and the door swung inwards, slamming against the wall.

A girl, no more than sixteen, was sitting on the toilet with her knees pulled up to her chest and her arms wrapped around them. Tear-soaked mascara streaked her face. She stared silently at Marshall.

'And I'll blow your house in,' he said, grinning.

14

Jimmy pulled at the blinds on the window facing the street and looked out, still anxious that someone must have heard the gunfire. There was nothing out of the ordinary. Behind him, the girl sitting on the couch made a noise. He turned and watched as Marshall finished taping her mouth, wrapping the silver plumber's tape around her head several times. He had already bound her hands with the same tape.

The girl's name was Brianna Chalk and she was fifteen. They knew that much about her. She pulled in ragged breaths through her nose and huffed them out just as hard, mucus running from her nose over the tape.

'Calm down,' Jimmy told her. 'Breathe normally and you'll be fine.'

Her head snapped from side to side as she looked at him and then at Marshall. Her breathing became more laboured and Jimmy was worried she might pass out. It would be harder to move her if she was unconscious.

Jimmy knew what she was feeling. He had, what was the right word…an experience in jail that was not dissimilar. He didn't dwell on the memory, blinking once slowly to wipe it from his mind.

He walked to where the girl was sitting and kneeled in front of her, far enough away so that she would not be able to butt him if she decided that might be a good idea. Marshall backed away a couple of feet and stood behind Jimmy.

'I'm sorry about what happened to your parents,' Jimmy told her.

The girl's gaze went over Jimmy's shoulder to the body of her mother lying on the floor against the far wall.

'I don't expect you to believe me when I say that. But it's true.'

Marshall stared at the side of the girl's face, his head tilting a fraction to one side.

'Now,' Jimmy said, 'you need to calm down or you're going to faint. If you faint you're no good to us because you'll be immobile.'

The girl looked back at Jimmy.

'Do you understand what I'm telling you?' Jimmy asked.

She frowned and shook her head. Jimmy sighed and rubbed a hand over the top of his head.

'We need to take you with us,' he said. 'Only for a little while. Then we'll let you go somewhere safe. But we can only do that if you're still conscious.'

The girl nodded vigorously this time and squeezed tears from her eyes. Her face was a wet mess.

Jimmy told his brother to get a towel from the kitchen and, when he returned with it, Jimmy wiped the girl's face. He did his best to get the make-up streaked on her skin as clean as he could.

'You got a hooded sweatshirt or jacket you can wear?' Jimmy asked her when he was done.

She nodded.

Jimmy told his brother to go get something like that from the girl's room upstairs.

'We need to cover your hands and face,' Jimmy explained to her, 'so we can get you to the car outside without any drama.'

Her eyes widened again and her chin trembled. Jimmy put his hands on her cheeks and pulled her face forward until their noses almost touched.

'My brother doesn't react well to drama, as you can see. So if you keep calm, Brianna Chalk, we'll be cool.'

Marshall came into the room and held up a Patriots hoody like a kid showing his dad the gift he got that day.

15

She had just gone into the bathroom when her dad came home and shouted 'burgers'. Brianna Chalk looked at the small pill in her hand, still inside the plastic pouch Darnell had given to her after school.

'Take this then come see me,' he told her before kissing her and pushing his hand up inside her shirt for a quick grope.

She wasn't sure she liked Darnell that much, but what the hell. Anything was worth trying once if it helped erase the reality of her life.

Her dad was a constant reminder of how she didn't want her life to turn out. He worked as an accountant at some sort of electronics company with an office in a crummy building on the west side of Boston. She'd looked through the filing cabinet he kept in the bedroom once to find his payslip. From what she could tell, he made less than forty thousand a year. Her mom was a part time receptionist at another anonymous office.

They vacationed at the same place each year up in Maine. It was the most boring place she could have imagined, beside a lake that was more like a puddle and with no TV.

Brianna stuffed the pouch with the pill in the back pocket of her jeans when she heard her dad's voice. She turned to the mirror above the sink and pushed her hair back from her face. She knew that she was pretty; could tell that she got her looks from her mom from the old pictures she saw of her.

Her dark hair was long and naturally wavy. Her skin was largely free of blemishes notwithstanding the regular diet of fast food when her dad was late home – which was often. Her body was developing fast and it was the kind that boys seemed to like. Not just headcases like Darnell.

The sound of her mother shouting startled her. She whipped her head around as the first gunshot sounded. The others followed in quick succession. Brianna grabbed at the door handle, unlocked the door and pulled it open a fraction. She saw her father's body in the hall. His head was a bloody mess. She closed the door and locked it again, putting her back against the door and covering her mouth with her hand as the tears came. She didn't much like her dad, but he was still her dad. He called her 'babe' all the time, like he thought it made him seem younger.

The tears came harder.

The one called Jimmy drove the car while the other one sat beside Brianna in the back of the car. He held the gun in his lap, pointing at her belly. She knew that he kept looking at her but she avoided turning to him. There was something about him that scared her; made her feel as if he would not let her go if it was his decision.

The hooded sweatshirt had been pulled over her head with her hands still taped together in front of her. The empty sleeves hug loose by her side and she felt like she might pass out at any time. It was hot and stuffy in the car and it reeked of beer and body odour, like they lived in it.

She couldn't shake the image of her mother's body out of her head. All that blood. The worst part was her eyes, open but devoid of light or life.

The man next to her, Marshall, moved his leg until it touched hers. She felt the heat of his body through her jeans.

Brianna Chalk closed her eyes and prayed that the god she had long since forsaken would keep her safe.

16

Early spent the rest of the day at the sheriff's office writing up a report on his visit to the jail to see Manu Polite and recording the traffic tickets he had issued the previous week. That was the job. Everything had to be documented.

Kapnick came in to the deputies' room not long past four in the afternoon and told Frank Wood and Randolph Jones to attend a car accident five miles north on Highway 28. There was a suspected fatality and Early was glad to have missed the call. Jones was in his late forties and grumbled about the assignment. He complained about most things in life so his lack of enthusiasm came as no surprise.

Jones looked like a librarian. He was thin and no taller than five-seven. He wore his uniform more neatly than any law enforcement officer Early had seen in his career. Jones pushed a pair of square spectacles up his nose and sighed as he stood and put his hat on. Kapnick stayed in the deputies' room until Wood and Jones left.

Early waited for the sheriff to say what was on his mind. He wasn't a man to share much by way of friendly conversation with his deputies.

'Why don't you head home now,' Kapnick said, looking at his watch. 'Not much happening anyway.'

'The boys might need help once they get out on the highway.'

Kapnick shook his head and smiled, running a hand over his moustache.

'You know, I think you are the only man I've met that would turn down a chance to get some time off.'

Early shrugged.

'Go home,' Kapnick said.

Early held his boss's gaze for a moment. He said 'okay', turned off his computer and left. Kapnick stood in the doorway of the room and watched Early all the way out of the building.

Home for Early was a one bedroom wood cabin beside Briar Pond that was accessed via a dirt track off of Briar Street. The entrance to the track was opposite a Holiday Inn and Early ate at the steak and seafood restaurant there often enough that the waiters knew his name. Early's dad used to call his house the shack, back when he remembered. Early did not mind, he loved its simplicity.

Early's police cruiser bounced along the track for a half-mile after the turn-off before the house became visible through the trees that lined Briar Pond. It was a single storey cabin with no boundary fence and a shelter for one car attached to its left-hand side. The cabin had previously been owned by the town and used as really no more than a store for fishing gear when Early bought it. The place had been a mess but he'd worked hard on it with his dad's help for a couple of years when he wasn't in uniform: building the car shelter; upgrading the windows and doors; installing a new kitchen and bathroom and erecting porches front and back that ran the full length of the house. He liked to sit on the back porch at night with a beer and a book. If he looked hard enough through the trees, he could see the edge of the pond from there.

Inside, the cabin was furnished sparingly with a big sofa and a single armchair in front of a stone fireplace in the living room. The kitchen was separated from that room by a counter and double glass doors led off the kitchen onto the back porch. A door off the living room led along a short hallway to the bedroom and bathroom. Early was not a fan of the wooden walls inside the house and so had lined the interior of the cabin with drywall, plastered it and painted it all white.

Early took a shower and changed into jeans and an old t-shirt. He cooked some eggs and toast, topped it with grilled tomato and grabbed a beer from the fridge before heading out to the back porch. He ate the food from the plate on his lap and finished the beer in three long pulls.

He had first noticed his dad's symptoms when they had shared a beer on that porch. It was supposed to be a celebration of sorts, having completed all of the major work on the house, on one of those perfect New England nights with the sun bleeding into the horizon. His dad started talking about being in town earlier that week and running into a friend of his. Early had turned to look at his father, aware that this was a friend who had died some years ago from a heart attack. His dad stopped mid-sentence after a minute or so. He looked at Early with an embarrassed smile and took a drink of his beer.

It went downhill from there.

17

Early figured he had dozed off for an hour or so because the sun was lower in the sky when he was awoken by someone banging on his front door. He stood without thinking, sending his empty plate clattering onto the deck of the porch. He checked his watch and saw that it was after six.

Early padded barefoot to the front door and opened it. No one was there but a car was parked in front of the house. It looked familiar to him but he could not place it immediately. Early stepped onto the porch and looked to his right. Kate Foley was at the far end of the porch looking around the side of the house. She was dressed in a pair of beige shorts with white sneakers and a pale blue cotton shirt. Her hair was tied up and she was holding onto the corner of the house as she strained to look around the side. Early watched her, saying nothing. A smile formed on his face.

Kate turned back to the front of the house. She was startled to see Early and held her hand to her chest while taking in a sharp breath. Early laughed.

'Jesus, Early,' she said, striding towards him. 'You scared the crap out of me.'

'Sorry.'

She slapped lightly at one of his arms when she reached him.

'Why didn't you say something?'

He shrugged and told her to come inside.

'You want something to drink?' he asked, closing the

door behind her.

Kate paused, looking around the cabin and turning to face Early.

'Place looks nice,' she said.

'You don't have to look so surprised. What did you expect?'

'I don't know. Not…this.'

She waved a hand in the air.

'What? Moose heads on the wall and bearskin on the floor.'

She narrowed her eyes at him.

'You know what I meant,' she said.

Early went past her to the kitchen.

'Drink?' he asked.

'Just a Coke or something.'

Early took a can from the fridge and poured it into a glass for her. He watched as Kate sat gingerly on the on the sofa, still sore from her injuries. She self-consciously put a hand to her face where she had done her best to cover the bruising with make-up. She glanced at him and he quickly looked down, emptying the can and walking around the counter to hand her the glass. He leaned against the fireplace as she took a drink. He was struck by how good she looked with her hair pulled back off her face.

'How did you find this place?' Early asked.

'I called the office. Shirley Lee told me this was where you lived.'

'She's helpful that way.'

Kate held the glass in both hands on her lap and looked out of the front window. It was an overly formal posture, like she was uncomfortable.

'What can I do for you, Kate?' Early asked.

She put the glass down on the floor at her feet and spoke without making eye contact.

'How was my dad with you? I mean, earlier. When you came to the house.'

'He was fine. Why?'

She ran her hands back from her face as if to smooth her hair.

'That's good.'

Early sat in the armchair and leaned forward, resting his arms on his knees.

'What's this about, Kate?'

She stood up, nudging the glass and spilling some of her drink on the floor. She looked down at the glass and then walked to the front window, crossing her arms and staring out at nothing.

Early sat back in his chair. He guessed that she had something to say and would get to it in her own time.

'He didn't say *anything* to you? My dad.'

'Anything like what?'

She turned to face him, leaning back against the wall beside the window.

'I don't know. Anything bad or…'

'Listen, your dad and I understood each other right from the start.'

'What does that mean?'

'I don't think he liked me back when we dated. And his opinion probably hasn't changed that much.'

'He told you that?'

'No. But it was pretty clear from the way he spoke to me and behaved when I was around you. He was always sort of cold towards me.'

'You never said.'

Early shrugged.

'I guess most dads don't like their daughter's boyfriends.'

'What about at the trial? You know, when the school got sued by that kid's parents.'

Early felt his face flush. Kate watched, unsure if he was feeling anger or shame or something else. He had never spoken to her about his feelings after what happened. Never spoke to anyone about it so far as she could tell. He gave up on football and retreated into himself.

'My dad acted for the family in the lawsuit,' she said. 'You must have spoken to him, right?'

'It settled on the morning of the trial, you know that. We never got started. The school's insurance company paid out.'

'But…'

'I never spoke to him. I mean, I gave a deposition about what happened but he wasn't there. One of his partners covered it. I guess he felt too close to it. Too close to me.'

Kate walked back to the sofa and sat at the end closest to the armchair.

'You know, he refused to talk to me about the lawsuit. I asked him, like, a hundred times.'

'You were at college by then. We weren't together.'

'That wasn't my choice. Us not being together, I mean.'

He looked at her and felt the years fall away. He remembered that day she had come to see him before going to college. Remembered how he had wanted to grab her and hold on. To tell her that he needed her.

'You know,' Kate said, holding his gaze, 'I told my dad after you left today that this wouldn't have happened to me if we had stayed together.'

Early said nothing.

'He said it wouldn't have made him like you any more.'

Early leaned forward and pushed a loose stand of hair off of her cheek and behind her ear. The bruising around her eye was more prominent this close. He felt a surge of anger, wanting to hit something. Hit it hard.

'If I asked you to help me,' she said, 'what would you do?'

Early took a breath and sat back in the chair.

'I'd call someone in Boston. Is that what you want?'

'No.'

Early shook his head and stood. He went to the kitchen and grabbed a handful of tissues to mop up the spilled drink.

'I should go,' Kate said, standing.

Early stayed in the kitchen, leaning on the counter top.

'Did you come here for a different answer?' he asked.

She smiled thinly and looked at a framed photograph

sitting on top of the fireplace. It was an old photo of Early in his football uniform standing between his parents with his arms around their shoulders. They all looked so happy, as if life would never be better than in that moment. Maybe it wasn't.

She thought of her own wedding photo and felt nauseous.

'I really don't know why I came.'

She walked to the front door and pulled it open.

'Is this like the last time?' she asked. 'We go our separate ways.'

Early stood where he was.

'You're married, Kate.'

That thin smile returned.

'So I am,' she said.

Early stared at the door after she left, listening to the sound of her car as it disappeared down the track.

18

She watched the cabin grow more distant in the rear-view mirror as the car heaved and bumped down the dirt track. A bend in the track pushed it out of sight and there was nothing but woodland to look at.

Kate stopped at the end of the track as cars passed in front of her on Briar Street. Early's question rattled around in her head. She wasn't sure why she had gone to the house, or what she had expected from him. She put her head back against the seat and closed her eyes. She gripped the steering wheel tighter and rolled her hands over it as the screen of her cell phone glowed brightly. Her husband's face appeared on the screen with his number underneath. She stared at it for a moment, unsure what to do. She was struck again by her physical attraction to him: his dark hair, slender nose and brown eyes. But the thought of any further intimacy with him brought the nausea back.

The screen of her phone faded to black as the call ended. Kate let out a sigh, unaware that she had been holding her breath.

The phone rang again. Kate picked it up, feeling a surge of anger at seeing his face again.

'What is it, John?' she asked when she answered the call, glancing in her mirror again.

He didn't say anything. She could hear a TV or radio somewhere in the background and wondered where he was. She stared at the hotel across the street and a thought hit her that he might be watching her. She scanned the windows facing the street but saw no one.

'If you're prepared to be an adult about this we can talk, John. Otherwise…'

'Kate?'

He sounded different, his voice higher than normal. There was a rasp to it, as if he was hoarse from shouting.

'What? You called me.'

'I called you.'

He was being a dick. She thought about hanging up.

'Sorry,' he said. 'Yeah, I called you. How was your day?'

Kate held the phone out in front of her and stared at his picture on the screen.

'What are you doing?' she asked, putting the phone back to her ear.

'What do you mean?'

That weird, fluty voice of his was starting to unnerve her.

'Why did you call, John?'

'Just checking in, you know. Seeing how you're doing. I mean, I miss you.'

She wondered if he was doing this to somehow craft a defence if she reported him to the police – her lawyer brain taking over.

'Are you recording this call? Because if you are, I don't appreciate…'

'No, of course not. What do you mean? Why are you being like this?'

Kate laughed – though it came out sounding more like a snort.

'I'm going to hang up now,' she said.

'Jesus, Kate. I'm just…' his voice went higher still, cutting off abruptly.

She kept the phone pressed to her ear but all she could hear now was that distant TV. When he spoke again, he voice was much lower.

'I'll see you soon, sweetheart.'

The connection went dead. Kate dropped the phone on

the seat next to her, feeling very alone. She looked in the mirror again hoping to see Early standing there. But there was no one.

19

John Lustig stared at the TV that was on in the corner with the volume turned low. He placed his cell phone carefully on the arm of his chair. The smell of burned food from earlier still lingered in the apartment.

Who was that on the phone?

His head was still cloudy. He'd had a shower after the incident with the burnt bacon and the smashed-up smoke alarm and tried unsuccessfully to sleep – restlessly turning on his bed.

The TV had not helped. Talking heads shouting at each other and kids young enough to be his own shooting each other dead in the streets.

He reached down to the floor and picked up the handgun. He'd cleaned and oiled it before his shower and he could smell the tang of metal when he held it close to his face.

He grabbed the phone with his free hand and scrolled through his contacts until he found the number he was looking for. Joe Foley, Kate's dad, answered on the third ring.

'Hey, Joe. I'm looking for Kate. Is she there?'

Joe Foley paused before speaking.

'It's not appropriate that you call here, John. I mean, given the circumstances.'

Lustig frowned in the near dark of his apartment, light from the TV flickering across his face as the images changed.

'Do you hear me?' Joe Foley asked.

'I hear you.'

'Kate may not have called the cops on you but I have. And I'll do it again you son of a bitch.'

It came out in fast, like it was one word: *sonofabitch.*

'I don't know what's wrong Joe. Can I speak to Kate?'

'This conversation is over. Don't come anywhere near this house or my daughter, you understand.'

'So she is there?'

The dial tone sounded.

Lustig tapped the barrel of the gun against the screen of his phone where Joe Foley's face was still displayed.

'I'll go wherever I fucking please,' Lustig told the phone.

20

It was near dark when Jimmy Cain turned onto Sandy Pond Road at the south end of Great Herring Pond, a few miles north of Cape Cod. He had driven south after what happened at the house, unsure what to do. He watched his brother closely in the mirror, seeing him stare at the girl for too long sometimes. The girl ignored him. She cried a couple of times but otherwise was quiet.

He drove to put distance between them and the house, wanting to stay within the state because it was familiar territory for him. He didn't want to be somewhere unknown if there came a time when he needed to know the terrain.

They drove along the road flanked by dense woodland. The lights from two houses set back from the road on either side passed quickly. He looked at the one on his left and caught a quick glimpse of a big, modern structure. There was a lot of glass and light. He looked in the mirror and saw that Marshall had fallen asleep, his head tilted towards the girl. She had shuffled over in her seat as far as she could, but there was still a good deal of contact with Marshall. She had her head turned, looking out of the window.

Jimmy drove on for another half mile with no sign of any other houses. He turned onto a double width dirt track on his left and drove until he reached the end – a circular turning point enclosed by a wall of trees. He pulled the car around until it faced back up the road, turned in his seat and looked at the girl.

'We're going to stay here for the night.'

She looked sideways at him and back out of the window. Jimmy didn't know what else to say. He looked at the side of her face and at his brother. The girl turned and watched him, her body shrinking back against the seat.

Jimmy reached back and grabbed his brother's arm, shaking it lightly. Marshall opened his eyes slowly, taking a few moments to comprehend where he was.

'We stopping here?' he asked, stretching his arms above his head.

Jimmy nodded.

Marshall opened the door nearest to him and moved to get out.

'I need a piss,' he said, walking away from the car and disappearing behind one of the trees lining the track.

He left the car door open and Jimmy could hear the warm splash of his brother's bladder emptying on the ground.

'Do you need to go?' Jimmy asked the girl.

She nodded, her eyes darting to the open door.

'We'll stay back and let you do your business,' Jimmy said. 'But don't run, okay.'

She said okay, her voice stronger than Jimmy had expected. He turned back to look out of the windscreen, wondering if the girl had a reserve of strength that he would have to worry about. He had told her they would let her go so that she would cooperate, without thinking about how it would play out in the end. He closed his eyes and thought about killing her to see how it made him feel.

In his mind, he pushed her ahead of him as they walked into the woods and shot her in the back of the head. He didn't want any of that screaming and pleading if he got her to go down on her knees. She'd know what he was going to do at that point. Better to do it fast, before the realisation came to her.

He found it difficult to feel anything. Maybe it was like that until you had to do it. He thought that he'd be okay about it.

Jimmy opened his eyes as Marshall got back in the car and slammed the door hard. Marshall pulled at the crotch of his jeans.

'She needs to go,' Jimmy said. 'You stay here and I'll take her.'

Marshall didn't react. Jimmy knew two things: that his brother was not happy about the course of events he had just outlined; and that he would accept it without complaint.

Jimmy kept the car engine running and the lights on. He wanted to see where he was going and also wanted to get the car moving again in a hurry if need be.

The air was cool with light cloud covering the sky and the residual heat of the day ebbing. Jimmy stretched and breathed deep, glad to be out of the car and in the open air. His own bladder felt full, the pressure uncomfortable on his groin. He looked at the car and thought about which was worse, leaving Marshall in the car with the girl or letting his brother take her into the woods to do her business. It was an easy choice.

Jimmy grabbed his gun from the floor of the car under the steering wheel and jammed it into the front of his jeans. He went to the rear door of the car, opened it and motioned with his hand for the girl to get out. He looked up the track as the last vestiges of daylight faded. The world seemed to close in on him.

The girl swung her legs out of the car and held her bound hands out, looking up at Jimmy.

'I need to use my hands,' she said. 'Unless you want to help me.'

Jimmy rubbed at his chin, feeling stubble developing into a beard. He leaned forward and grabbed her hands, pulling her upright.

'I'll help,' he told her, pushing the hood back off her head.

She stared at him and, for the first time, he noticed how pretty she was; became more aware of the fullness of her breasts pressing against the cloth of her top. He hadn't been this close to a woman in a while. Sometimes looking out for Marshall left him with no space for himself. He rested one hand on the gun.

When his eyes came back up to the girl's face he saw a flicker of something, maybe a smile. But it was gone before he could fully register it.

21

It was always the way, Brianna Chalk, thought. Sooner or later they end up looking at your tits. He was trying to be all cool and noble, but it was so obvious the way he put his hand on the gun when he was staring. Like he wanted her to think that he was above all of that. She knew different.

When it came right down to it, they were all the same.

But there was nothing she could do while her hands were tied. She recognised the confusion that the woods would cause at night if she could just get in there without them following too close. She'd also seen the big house about a half-mile back. If she could get there, she might be safe.

The one called Jimmy grabbed her hands and pulled her up from the car seat. When she was standing he took the gun from his jeans and pointed towards the edge of the clearing. She saw a faint bulge in his jeans and turned to walk the way he had indicated.

The trees didn't seem quite so close together once they were in them. She moved between them and kept walking until he told her to stop. When she turned, he was looking back towards the car and tapping the barrel of the gun against the outside of his leg. A jolt passed through her as the thought struck her that he only brought her here to kill her.

He turned and looked at her for a long moment, like he was thinking what to do. Brianna willed herself not to cry, not to scream and plead with him. It took all of her effort to hold it together.

Finally, he reached around and put the gun into his rear waistband and walked towards her. He grabbed her hands and squeezed hard, staring into her eyes.

'I really don't want to hurt you,' Jimmy said. 'But you look like trouble, girl. And that's going to be bad for you if it turns out I'm right.'

She held his gaze for as long as she could before looking down.

'I won't be any trouble,' her voice wavered

She wasn't sure if he would recognise the lack of genuine emotion. He appeared to make a decision, grabbed at the end of the tape and unwound it. When he was done, she rubbed her wrists. She was about to say thanks when he pushed one hand into her throat and drove her back against the nearest tree. Her head hit hard and she tasted blood in her mouth as she bit the end of her tongue.

He pressed the gun to her mouth, splitting her bottom lip and drawing more blood. She tried to cry out, but his grip was too strong, robbing her of breath.

'I see you, Brianna,' he hissed at her. 'Don't think that I don't.'

Tears welled in her eyes and spilled down her cheeks. He smelled like cheap soap.

The gun was pushed up against her teeth and she opened her mouth to avoid them getting cracked and broken. He forced the gun deep into her mouth and her vision blurred as she struggled to get oxygen into her lungs.

He pressed his body against her and she could feel him growing down there. She reached up and lightly held his arms, trying to plead with her eyes as darkness encroached on her vision.

And then he stepped back and dropped the hand holding the gun to his side. Brianna doubled over and raggedly drew air in, tears streaming down her face and splashing onto the loose bark and twigs covering the dirt.

She was aware of him watching her until she got her

breathing under control. When she stood upright he was looking up at the sky as the cloud cover broke and a sliver of cold, blue light edged through.

'Do your business,' he said without looking at her.

I have to get out of here, she thought. Because If I don't, they *will* kill me.

22

Early found it difficult to concentrate on much of anything after Kate's visit. He remained uncertain as to the purpose of her coming to see him. Part of him hoped it was simply to be in the same room as him. He found it easy to slip back into her company after the many years that had passed since they had been together.

He watched TV for an hour, flicking between things and not settling on any one of them. After that, he took his weights out to the back yard with a view to pushing hard and sweating it all out. That worked for a while but left him unfulfilled.

When he was done working out, he wiped his body down with a towel and went for a shower. All that did was bring the memories back in a rush, memories of the day that boy died.

His name was Jerod Butler. He was slightly built for a football player but moved faster than anyone Early had seen play at high school level. He received the opening kick-off and cut right through the heart of Early's team, taking it all the way for a touchdown. After that, he faced the sideline where Early and his teammates stood watching, puffing his chest and thumping a fist against his breastbone.

At that moment, eighteen-year-old Early Simms wanted to put him onto the ground so hard that he could feel his muscles tingle.

It was a hot Friday night with the dirt of the field packed hard. Every play brought a cloud of dust from the field as the players' cleats dug ruts into the earth. By half time, Early's jersey was soaked with sweat and he was breathing harder than he had all season long. Jerod Butler turned out to be the star player for the opposition – lining up at both running back and wide receiver and gouging the defence for something like fifteen yards on every play when he had the ball in his hands. Early had been left grasping at air at the back of the boy's heels on several occasions. His team trailed by fourteen at the half.

In the locker room at half-time, Early sat on a wooden bench some way distant from his teammates feeling frustrated and increasingly angry. His anger was not directed so much at Butler's abilities, but at the constant jibes he aimed at Early and his teammates.

'What's wrong with you, Simms?' his coach shouted at him. 'Not interested in playing today, son. Too busy crying.'

Early stood and threw his helmet onto the floor. The loud crack made everyone in the locker room turn to stare at him.

'That's it,' the coach said. 'I want all of you fucking mad. This guy is making fools of you. Somebody needs to hit him out of his socks.'

Early clearly remembered his coach staring at him for a beat.

'You up to the job, Simms?'

Early took a deep breath and wiped sweat from his face with a towel.

'Yes, sir, I'm ready.'

It happened five minutes into the second-half of the game. Butler came through a hole in the line and into Early's domain as middle linebacker. He'd seen the formation that the opposition had used once before in the first half and gambled that the coach had gotten lazy and called the same play. He was right.

Butler came through the space between his offensive linemen with his eyes wide, thinking that he was about to go a long way, maybe even score again.

Early came at him from the side, moving at close to full speed and lowering his shoulders ready to burst up into the tackle. Butler saw him late and put his head down as if he thought he could take Early head on.

Early's shoulder pad connected square with the top of Butler's helmet, compressing and breaking his spine. Everyone heard it. A collective gasp came from the crowd around the field.

It was a clean, legal tackle. One that Early had put his whole body into. That was the game of football.

It was Early's last game.

He met Kate after the game, long after everyone else had gone home. After the medical examiner had left with Jerod Butler's body.

She held him tight for an age, her head pressed against his chest. He wrapped his arms around her and cried. She waited for him, giving him as long as he needed. His hair hung long back then and when she looked up at him his eyes were obscured by it. She took both hands and pushed his hair off his face, then wiped the damp from his cheeks.

She told him that it wasn't his fault.

He said he knew that, but his voice lacked conviction.

They went back to her house, the one on Oyster Road. Her parents were out for the night at a dinner for some local business organisation that her father chaired. Early was a mess so she told him to take another shower. He allowed her to lead him to the bathroom where he stood listlessly as she peeled off his sweat-soaked clothes.

His shoulder, the one he had used to hit Jerod Butler, was already starting to bruise. Kate put her hand on it lightly. Early looked and saw the bruise. Kate went up on her toes and kissed the discoloured skin, her hands resting on his chest. Early pushed her back against the bathroom wall and clawed at her clothes, pulling them off as fast as he could.

'Not here,' she told him, grabbing his hands. 'Not like this.'

Kate took his hands and led him to the shower. She turned it on for him, putting the heat up high. Early let her do it, his muscles gone slack again.

When he was finished in the shower, Early wrapped a towel around his waist and went to Kate's room. She was waiting for him, sitting on the edge of the bed with a sheet pulled up above her breasts. He stopped inside the doorway. The window was open and the smell of the sea permeated the room, the curtains moving lightly in the breeze. The only light came from the sun as it dipped slowly into the sea, the room glowing a warm yellow.

Kate stood and let the sheet fall to the floor. She was naked underneath. She walked to Early and led him to the bed. He waited while she removed his towel and kissed him on the mouth, trying to make the ice in his blood melt with her warmth.

She pushed him onto the bed and straddled him, kissing him as deeply as she ever had.

When they had made love, Early lay looking up at the ceiling and letting the cool air from the window flow across his body. Kate lay beside him, propped up on her elbow.

'I love you, Early,' she said.

He knew that she did.

He wanted to tell her the same, but could not.

Early sat alone in his living room and stared at the blank TV screen. He had regrets in his life. Everyone did. But that last night with Kate had stayed with him through many years of relationships with women that never lasted any longer than nine months. He thought that he had become content with his own company over the last year, throwing himself into his work and looking after his dad before he went into the home. Perhaps he had been fooling himself. Kate's re-entry to his life had changed things. He realised now how alive she made him feel.

He wondered if it was the same for her.

23

Joe Foley was waiting for his daughter when she got home. He was in the thinking chair with a book open on his lap.

'Where's mom?' Kate asked.

Her father's eyes looked up.

'She went to bed.'

Kate looked at her watch. It was too soon for her mother to be in bed. Joe Foley closed his book and put it on the floor beside his chair.

'She's not coping well,' he told Kate.

She moved into the room and sat on the couch.

'Coping with what, Dad? I'm fine.'

Kate had her phone in her hands, turning it and glancing down at it often. Her father watched her quietly.

'What?' she said, trying to sound exasperated but coming off as defensive.

'Did John call you tonight?'

She frowned and shook her head.

'What do you mean?'

Her dad leaned back in his chair, his hands resting on his thighs. He turned his head to look out of the window.

'It's a simple question, Kate,' he said. 'I mean, I don't think it needs much of an explanation.'

Kate sat back on the couch, stuffing the phone into one of the pockets of her shorts.

'Did he call here too?'

Her father nodded.

'I'm worried about you,' he told her. 'John sounded…odd.'

'I know.'

'Is he dangerous?'

'You mean apart from when he did this to my face?'

'I'm serious. And you should be too. You're the one that deals with criminals all day long.'

'He's not who I thought he was.'

'That much is obvious, Kate. But the real question is: who is he really? I mean, is he capable of more? Of worse.'

Kate bit her lower lip.

'I honestly don't know, Dad.'

'You should call the police in Boston and report this properly. They'll pick him up.'

'That won't solve the problem. He'll be out inside a day and probably even more pissed at me for having him arrested.'

Joe Foley sighed and tugged at an ear. Kate knew her dad well. It was a sign that he was unhappy at not getting his own way. She walked over to him and sat on the arm of the chair, taking one of his hands and clasping it in hers.

'What did he say when he called?'

'Nothing. That's the problem. He was weirdly polite and didn't even acknowledge that anything was wrong.'

'Did he know I was here?'

'Where else would you be?'

Kate patted her dad's hand and smiled at him.

'Will you think about it?' he asked her. 'I mean, making a formal complaint about John.'

'I will.'

Kate leaned down and kissed her father's cheek, telling him that she was going to soak in a bath. She was at the doorway when he spoke again.

'Where did you go tonight?'

She turned to look at him.

'For a drive. You know, just to get out.'

He nodded slowly.

'Did that drive take you anywhere near Early Simms?'

She said nothing, preferring the silence to lying to her father.

'Be careful, Kate. These things…'

He didn't finish the thought.

'I know, Dad.'

24

It was quiet in the car, the only sounds being the deep breathing of the two men. Brianna Chalk looked at the one called Marshall sitting beside her. He was slumped away from her on the seat, his mouth hanging open. The other one had bound her wrists in the same piece of tape after she had finished peeing out in the woods. It wasn't as tight as it had been but she still could not completely loosen it as she moved her hands back and forward.

She had not been able to sleep after coming back to the car, certain that she would not be leaving the company of these two men alive. It both terrified and fortified her. She had to find a way out. The big house down the road loomed large in her memory.

The car doors were locked but she could pull the pin up on her door and open it. She knew that she would not be fast enough or able to get away while her hands were tied. For the last hour she had been running an idea through her head. She decided that it was the best chance she had.

Brianna put her hands in her hair and tousled it, bowing her head and shaking it slightly to add to the effect. She nudged Marshall's knee with her own. He did not stir. She did it again, a little harder, leaving her leg touching his. His mouth clamped shut and his head snapped up. He looked around the car with a frown until his eyes found her. He was still half-asleep. That's what she was hoping. She wasn't certain of the time, but it was well after midnight and his exhaustion was the best weapon she had.

'I need to use my hands,' she whispered, pushing her leg harder against his.

He looked down at her leg and rubbed at an eye with his hand. Brianna glanced at the other man in the front of the car. His breathing remained deep and even.

Brianna decided that she didn't have much time. This had to be quick.

She moved closer to Marshall and leaned in to kiss him. His eyes remained barely open and he watched her drowsily all the way in till she touched her lips to his, flicking her tongue out softly. Her hands rested on his thigh.

'I need my hands,' she repeated, her mouth close to his.

Marshall pressed one hand against her breast and squeezed, looking down as he did it.

Brianna brought her hands up, pushing him off of her. She bit the inside of her cheek to stop from screaming. Her stomach roiled.

'Not here,' she whispered.

His eyes were wide open.

'Out there,' she said. 'Where *he* can't hear.'

She knew Marshall wanted her and hoped that desire was stronger than the bond he had with the other man. She was pretty sure it was.

Marshall looked at Jimmy still asleep in the front of the car. He turned back to Brianna and put his mouth on hers, opening it and searching her mouth with his tongue. Brianna grabbed at his shirt, hoping that he would read it as desire.

She pulled away from him and held her hands up again.

Jimmy didn't move.

'You want my hands free don't you?'

She bit her bottom lip for added effect. Men could be such suckers if they thought they could get into her pants.

Marshall looked quickly at Jimmy again, seeming to come to a decision. He grabbed the end of the tape and started to unwind it. Brianna tried to keep excitement in check. When he was finished he put the tape onto the floor at his feet.

'Outside,' Brianna said, looking once more at Jimmy before pulling up the lock on her door and turning to push it open.

She felt the cool night air on her face, momentarily closing her eyes and seeing freedom. She felt Marshall's hand on her shoulder and bolted up and out of the car, slamming the door closed behind her, hearing the thunk of the door hitting Marshall. She didn't look back; didn't dare to.

She heard Marshall shout, the sound starting low and rising to a feral scream.

Heard the other door open as Jimmy got out of the car.

Then she was in the woods.

25

The sky was mostly clear but the moon's light was filtered to little more than that of a flickering candle under the canopy of leaves. Brianna ran as fast as she could, feeling her thighs and lungs start to burn after no more than fifty yards. She cursed herself for having lost interest in any form of sport or exercise. She held her hands up to push low branches out of her face and kept moving in the direction she figured that big house was. Tears streaked her cheeks, though she was unaware of them.

In the moment when Marshall screamed, Jimmy bolted upright. For a brief instant he thought that he was back in the old house. That night Marshall fell. His head whipped round towards the sound of his brother's fury and he saw the girl disappearing into the woods.

Jimmy fumbled on the floor for his gun, grabbed it and ran after the girl. Marshall was far slower than Jimmy and lagged behind, his breath ragged and harsh. Jimmy still had some of the old grace and power he had developed as a ball player and moved quickly through the trees. He could hear the girl crashing through the foliage and sobbing as she ran. There was no way she would be able to outrun him. Jimmy increased his speed, going as fast as the terrain would allow.

He didn't notice the sound of the girl's progress stopping. Didn't see the lump of wood she brought round from behind the tree until it hit him square on the bridge of the nose. The wood broke across Jimmy's face and his legs went out from under him. Sparkles danced in Jimmy's vision. He was vaguely aware of someone standing over him.

Brianna dropped the remains of the piece of wood and spat into Jimmy's face. Blood was streaming from his nostrils and the gash across his nose. She could tell that it was broken. His eyes were open but unfocused. She screamed 'motherfucker' at him and ran.

Jimmy found it difficult to coordinate his movements. He tried to wipe at the blood smearing his vision but couldn't seem to find his face. He could feel his throat filling with blood and choked to catch his breath.

Somebody knelt beside Jimmy and pulled him onto his side. Jimmy vomited blood and fast food remains onto the ground. Marshall crouched beside him, absently patting his arm and repeating his name.

Jimmy's head started to clear. He rolled onto his front and tried to push himself upright with his arms but he could not find the strength to do it. He lay on the ground, the smell of the woods and his own blood thick in his nostrils. The pain started to pulse in waves. Jimmy squeezed his eyes tight shut and spat more blood onto the ground.

Brianna kept running though she found it difficult now to lift her feet as she moved. Her face felt raw from the cuts that low branches had inflicted on her. She had lost all thought of protecting her face, her hands wind-milling at her sides to keep her from falling as the soft earth seemed to grab and pull at her feet.

Then she was clear of the trees, the shock of the open space and firmer ground causing her to stumble and fall forward. She huffed out a breath as she hit the ground and looked up to see a tarmac driveway ahead of her and, to her right, the dark outline of the house.

'Get up, Brianna,' she told herself, pushing up and

running onto the driveway and towards the sanctuary of the house.

26

Hank and Missy Applegate thought that they had life figured out until the night Brianna Chalk brought hell to their door. Hank was one of Plymouth's best known businessmen, running a successful private security contracting business. With the conflicts in Afghanistan and Iraq, the money had been rolling in for ten years or more as American firms working on contracts needed protection for their men in the field.

Hank had served with the Navy on nuclear submarines before retiring from a life underwater to see more of his family after their son, Jordan, was born. The boy was eighteen now and Hank hoped that he would take over the business some day and allow his old man to retire for good before it got too late to enjoy life.

Missy had been a real catch for Hank; everybody told him that. It got so he wanted to tell them to go to hell, but mostly he grinned through it. She was from upstate New York, smart and beautiful. Her family had enough money that she never had to worry about the good things in life. Hank still didn't know how a woman like that, and one as good-looking as Missy, had ever fallen for him. Hank was a tall man at over six-three and kept in good shape. But he always considered himself a little goofy looking with a big jaw and chin and a wide forehead. Missy was five-three and petite. She liked it when he picked her up and pulled her to his face to kiss her.

The early years of their marriage were rough with Hank away on duty for months at a time. It got harder after Jordan came along. Hank got close to screwing a female crew member after a drunken night out to celebrate the end of a long tour. It didn't happen and the close call persuaded Hank that he needed to be at home or Missy would walk. It was the best decision he ever made.

Missy had spotted the land where their house now sat by accident. She had gotten lost and turned onto Sandy Pond Road looking to find someone to give her directions. The first house she came across had a plot of land over the road where the owners kept their boats in a ramshackle wooden boathouse. A single horse wandered aimlessly in a field next to the boathouse. The 'for sale' sign immediately caught Missy's eye.

Eighteen months later and the house had been finished – a testament to modern urban architecture in concrete and glass. Missy liked nothing more than getting up early in the summer and doing thirty lengths of the pool before breakfast, the sun sparkling on the clear water and warming her back. Hank often watched her from the bedroom window overlooking the pool. She knew he liked to watch her in the water. She would turn onto her back and see him there in his shorts, his stomach flat and his chest muscles rippling as he lifted a mug to sip his coffee.

Missy woke first. She heard a woman shouting and hammering on the front door, though she could not make out what was being said. She looked at the clock beside her bed and saw that it was after three in the morning. The woman kept banging away at the door. Missy thought maybe she was shouting for help, over and over.

Hank stirred and rolled onto his back. Missy put a hand on his chest and shook him until he propped himself up on his elbows.

'Wha-issit?' he slurred.

Missy stared at him.

'You can't hear that racket at the door?'

Hank blinked sleep from his eyes. The noise was slowing down, but remained at a persistent volume.

'Go see what it is,' Missy said.

Hank sighed and threw the bed sheet off. He swung his legs onto the floor and padded slowly to the closet on the far wall. Moonlight leaked into the room from the edges of blinds that covered the floor to ceiling window. The air conditioning hummed at a low level.

Hank opened the closet and reached up to a high shelf. He pulled a matt-black pump action shotgun from the shelf, checked that it was loaded and that the safety was engaged and went out onto the upper hall.

The hall overlooked a double height entrance foyer and was fronted by a glass balcony. Two heavy wooden doors marked the entrance to the house. There were wide glass panels both to the sides of the doors and above it. The noise had stopped before Hank came out of the bedroom. He stood still and listened, watching the doors.

A girl's face appeared to the left of the doors, her breath misting the glass and her fingers smudging the clean surface. She looked wild, her hair a mess and blood streaking her face. She cupped her hands to the glass and squinted into the foyer. Hank brought the shotgun up, holding it high across his chest with the barrel pointed at the floor. The movement caught the girl's attention. She looked up at Hank and started hammering on the glass.

'Let me in, please. Let me in.'

Hank looked out of the glass above the door at the driveway of the house and the woods beyond. He couldn't see anything.

When he looked back at the girl she had turned her head to look behind her.

'Two men,' she shouted when she turned back to Hank. 'Let me in.'

Hank wasn't about to open the door until he found out what this girl wanted. He moved along the hall to the stairs and started down, the shotgun still held across his chest.

'What is it, Hank?' Missy asked, looking out from behind the bedroom door.

Hank waved a hand at her, telling her to stay in the room.

'I don't know. Some crazy girl.'

Hank was surprised that Jordan had not woken and appeared from his room; probably something to do with getting home at 2:00 a.m.

The girl at the window turned to look behind her again. This time her head whipped around to face inside the house real fast.

'Ohmygod. Ohmygod. They're coming. Let me in.'

Hank thought that he saw movement behind the girl, but everything outside was indistinct in the dark.

Hank knew that the girl could be scamming him – that people might be waiting right there with her to invade their home as soon as he opened the door. But his instincts for trouble were pretty good; had to be given his line of work. He moved quickly down the last few stairs and unlocked the door, pulling it open and stepping back to let the girl in. She fell forward and scrabbled at the highly polished wooden floor, her feet slipping as she tried to stand. She gave up and shuffled backwards on her butt.

'Thank you, thank you, thank you,' she said, starting to cry.

Hank stepped outside and made a show of lifting the shotgun to point it at the end of the driveway.

'You fellas had better just turn around and get the hell out of here,' he shouted to the dark.

27

Early lay in bed staring at the ceiling, all too aware of time barely moving from the soft glow of digital clock on the table. He had tried to read a book but could not concentrate, the words blending together after a few minutes as his mind wandered.

'Screw it,' he said aloud, slipping out from under the covers and padding barefoot to the kitchen.

The light of the moon was muted behind the clouds. Early pulled the fridge open and took a long drink of orange juice straight from a carton; when you lived alone you didn't have to worry about how anyone else felt. He put the carton back and looked for something to eat. There was some leftover chicken and not much else. He needed to do a grocery run.

He liked it best at night here, when it got real quiet and all you could hear was the silence of the woods. He stood at the doors leading out into the back yard and wondered what Kate was doing right now. He knew it was dangerous to get involved with her after what happened with her husband.

Sometimes, life was like that. If you don't embrace danger from time to time, you never achieve anything worthwhile.

28

Jimmy Cain was belly down on the grass to the side of the driveway leading to the Applegate's front door. He had thought about letting loose a shot at the big guy that came out the house. But the dude was huge and looked like he meant business with that shotgun, so he lay as quietly as he could while rasping air in through his mouth and swallowing blood from his broken nose.

The big guy eventually went back in the house and closed the door. Jimmy was pretty sure he had not seen them lying there on the grass

'You okay, Marshall?' Jimmy asked, turning to his brother.

Every time Jimmy moved his head a fresh wave of pain and nausea surged through him. That bitch had got him real good. No doubt his nose was smashed to shit. He couldn't breathe through it, felt like his whole head was clogged with blood. He hawked some of it out of his throat and spat it onto the driveway.

'We got to get her, Jimmy,' Marshall said, too loud for Jimmy's liking.

Jimmy put a finger to his lips. Marshall stood up and pointed at the house.

'We can just go get her,' he told Jimmy.

Jimmy raised himself up on his knees and rested his hands on his thighs as another wave of pain coursed through him. He waited till it passed and slowly stood, coughing and spitting some more blood.

Marshall looked at his brother and tried to hide a smile behind his hand.

'The fuck is so funny, Marshall?'

'Your nose…'

Marshall pointed his gun at Jimmy's face. Jimmy jerked his head to the side.

'Jesus,' he said sharply. 'Don't point that thing at me.'

Marshall dropped his hand and looked chastened.

Jimmy knew that he had to make a decision right now that was going to change the lives of a whole lot of people. There wasn't really a choice was how he figured it. The guy from the house was too far away in the dark to have seen them. But the girl knew their faces.

And the only way to the girl was to go through the guy with the shotgun. Him and anyone else that might be in the house.

Once you stepped off the cliff, you had no option but to fall hard and fast all the way to the bottom.

'Let's go,' he said, waving Marshall forward.

29

The girl clawed her way up the stairs ahead of Hank Applegate. He walked slowly backwards, looking out the window at driveway. He was unaware of the knotted muscles in his jaw as he ground his teeth together. He heard his wife talking fast on the phone behind the bedroom door. He reckoned the cops would be, maybe, thirty minutes away.

'Dad, what the hell?'

Hank's son, Jordan, came out of his room and stared at the girl sitting on the floor at the top of the stairs. She had her back against the wall with her hands clamped tight over her mouth. Her eyes were wide and her chest heaved as she tried to breathe.

Hank thought that he saw movement at the end of the drive but could not be certain.

'Shit,' he said quietly.

'Dad…'

Hank glanced quickly at his son. He still saw the little boy that Jordan used to be. His brown hair was long and hung down over his ears and over his eyes. He wore only a pair of shorts. His body was not yet fully developed; more skinny than muscled.

'There might be men outside,' Hank told his son, 'and they could be coming to the house. They probably have guns. I think they…assaulted that girl. And they will be intent on finishing the job.'

Jordan looked down at the girl. She nodded her head

violently.

'I need you to go into my room and ask your mother to give you the handgun I keep there.'

Hank was glad that he had taken both Missy and Jordan to the gun range before now. He wanted them to know about guns and to respect them, even if they never had to use them.

'What?' Jordan asked, his voice sounding thin.

Hank turned and looked at his son, aware that in doing so he might miss seeing someone approach the house.

'Son, I need your help to defend our home. Do you understand?'

Jordan nodded, though Hank was certain that the full weight of the situation had not yet made itself fully known to his son. He made no move to get the gun.

'Go now,' Hank said, raising his voice.

Jordan nodded again and this time went past the girl and pushed open the door of his parents' bedroom.

Sweat started to bead on Hank's forehead.

30

Jimmy grabbed Marshall by the shoulder and ran towards the left corner of the house. He kept his eyes on the front door until they were out of the line of sight. Now he felt better. They had the advantage of the guy not knowing where they were or what they were doing.

Jimmy expected that the cops would be on their way. He had no idea how close the nearest station was but figured he didn't want to be here at the house more than ten or fifteen minutes from now.

Marshall was leaning against the wall breathing heavily. He looked at Jimmy and grinned. Jimmy pointed around the side of the house. Marshall nodded and followed Jimmy as he slipped around the corner, keeping his back to the wall. There were two small windows high on the wall. Jimmy watched for movement at the windows until they reached the back corner of the house. He saw nothing.

Jimmy crouched at the corner and quickly looked into the back yard. He saw the swimming pool surrounded by a wooden deck that continued to the back of the house. There was a whole lot of glass at the back: a set of folding doors leading to the deck and long windows above. A light was on in the room nearest the corner on the second floor. Jimmy figured it was the master bedroom. He guessed that the occupants of the house might retreat back there and wait for the cops.

Jimmy saw a decent sized rock on the neatly trimmed

grass at the side of the house. He moved quickly and grabbed it, feeling the weight of it in his hand.

Marshall looked at the rock and frowned at his brother.

'I'm going back around front. You count to thirty and then chuck this in the pool,' Jimmy whispered. 'To get their attention.'

Marshall nodded.

'You follow what I'm saying?' Jimmy asked his brother.

Marshall said that he sure did. Jimmy asked him to repeat the instructions, which he did.

'Good,' he said. 'That should get them to look out of the window up there. The one with the light on. When they do that, shoot the shit out of the window.'

Marshall liked that part of the plan. He grinned again and nodded.

Jimmy grabbed Marshall's jacket and pulled his brother's face close to him.

'Once you do that, get your ass back here out of sight and wait for me, okay?'

Marshall saluted.

'Yes, sir.'

'Tell me you understand.'

'Count to thirty. Throw the rock. Shoot like shit. Duck and cover.'

'It's not a game, Marshall. You understand that, right?'

Marshall nodded. Jimmy turned and ran to the front of the house.

31

Brianna Chalk followed the good-looking boy into his parents' bedroom. The house was like a palace compared to her place. The master bedroom had the same floor plate as her whole house. A trim, older woman stood on the far side of the bed with a telephone in her hand.

'They're on the way,' the woman said in a shaky voice. 'The cops, I mean.'

Brianna wasn't sure to whom she was talking. The boy said okay and then asked the woman where his dad's gun was. The woman argued with the boy for a moment before going to the closet and lifting a small box from the top shelf. She knelt on the floor and opened the box, pulling back a dark cloth to reveal the handgun inside. She put a magazine in the handle and pushed it into place with an audible click. The boy took it from her and looked at the door to the bedroom as the big guy with the shotgun came into the room. Brianna walked to the window facing the back of the property. She looked down and saw a pool shimmering in the moonlight. She caught her own ghostly reflection in the window and saw what a mess she was. She rubbed her hands over her face and pushed her hair back.

'The cops?' the guy asked.

The woman nodded.

'How long till they get here?'

'I don't know.'

The guy didn't look happy at that.

'It's not my fault, Hank,' the woman said, her voice going high and shaky.

'I know. I know.'

Brianna felt safe here. She didn't think those two losers from the car would try to take on the guy with the shotgun. And they would know that the cops were on the way.

She heard a noise outside, like someone just jumped in the pool, and turned to the window. The woman and the boy moved towards the window when they heard the noise.

The big guy shouted 'no'.

Brianna saw movement on the ground underneath the window.

32

Jimmy realised a too late that he should have checked how much ammunition he and Marshall had. But he was already at the front door and by his own count Marshall was just about to release the rock. A second later he heard it hit with a splash. He looked down and saw spots of his own blood on the ground, wiping his sleeve across his face and trying to ignore the pain.

Marshall started shooting.

Jimmy thought he could hear his brother laughing over the noise of the gun and the sound of breaking glass. Jimmy hit the window next to the front door with the butt of his gun, dropping glass onto the floor inside. He reached through the hole in the window and fumbled for the lock on the inside of the door. The gunfire from the back of the house stopped. He figured Marshall used all of his ammunition.

33

Hank couldn't stop his wife or son. It all happened too fast.

The window of the bedroom shattered and he heard the unmistakable sound of gunfire. Missy's head jerked back, blood spraying the wall above their bed. Jordan shouted and doubled over, grabbing at his stomach.

Hank started to move. Missy fell to the floor.

Jordan spasmed twice as bullets bit into his right leg and upper chest. He fell, curling up into a foetal position.

Hank shouted and fired out the window, aiming downwards. He racked the slide on the shotgun and fired three more times before going down on his belly and crawling to the open window. He looked over the edge and saw one of the men disappearing around the corner towards the front of the house.

Brianna Chalk crouched in the corner of the room, staring at Hank and his injured son lying not far from her feet.

34

Jimmy slipped out of his shoes and ran across the foyer, taking the stairs two at a time. He knew that he had to risk everything now and that speed and surprise were the keys. There was no point leaving here with someone that could identify him still breathing. He had to make sure the girl was dead.

He ran for the door with light showing underneath it and pushed it open, slamming it back against the wall.

The floor by the window was covered in blood and a boy lay there unmoving. A woman lay on the bed, blood streaking her hair and face. The big guy was kneeling beside the boy. Jimmy shot him twice. The man fell back, toppling out of the shattered window.

The girl screamed from her position in the corner. Jimmy hadn't noticed that she was there. He shot her. She fell sideways against the wall, her mouth open in an 'O' shape. Blood splattered her face and chin from where the bullet had torn into her neck. She put her hand to the wound and arterial blood sprayed out between her fingers. She slid down the wall and sat on the floor, the surprised look still on her face.

Marshall came into the room, walked past Jimmy and picked the shotgun up off the floor. Jimmy saw that the boy lying dead on the floor had a gun in his hand. There was a box on the floor in front of an open closet with three full magazines in it. Jimmy knelt by the boy and pried his fingers off the gun. He took the magazines from the box and shoved them in the back pocket of his jeans.

'I need ammo for this,' Marshall said brandishing the shotgun as if it was a trophy.

'Look in there,' Jimmy told him, pointing at the closet with his chin.

Marshall came out of the closet after a brief search with a box of shotgun shells. His face lit up like Christmas while two dead kids grew cold at his feet.

Jimmy knew then that he had lost the ability to feel any real human emotion.

35

The phone rang at eight thirty the next morning. Early answered on the second ring, washing the last of his breakfast down with a mouthful of coffee.

'Hey, Early, it's Shirley Lee. How are you this morning?'

'I'm just about ready to leave.'

'Going to see your dad?'

'Not today, no. Probably just come into the office. What's up?'

'You know a…'

Early heard paper being moved around on her desk.

'Here it is,' she said. 'Nick Lowe. Says he's an FBI.'

Early frowned. He hadn't heard from Lowe in more than six months.

'Sure I know him.'

'He called here looking specially for you. Wouldn't talk to anyone else. Not Kappy, not anyone. Didn't tell me what it was about either.'

Early could tell she was put out by that. He knew Shirley Lee well enough to understand that she was queen of her domain and didn't take kindly to being kept in the dark.

'You got a number for Nick?' Early asked.

She said that she did, gave it to him quickly and ended the call. Early finished his coffee and called the number. Lowe answered before the end of the first ring.

'Special Agent Lowe,' he said, sounding distracted.

Early could hear a lot of noise in the background: men

and women speaking loud and fast and car tyres rolling over tarmac. He thought he could also hear the faint *whup-whup* of a helicopter in the distance.

'It's Early Simms, Nick.'

'Hey, Early. How you doing?'

Early smiled. He and Nick Lowe had shared more than a few beers once upon a time and he remembered the man fondly.

'I'm fine. What can I do for you?'

'Bad business,' Lowe said. 'Real bad business.'

Early waited for him to elaborate.

'You know Sandy Pond Road?'

Early rubbed at his chin.

'No, can't say that I do.'

'It's at the south end of Great Herring Pond. Not that far from you.'

'Okay.'

'Can you find it?'

'Sure. Listen Nick, what's this about?'

Someone said Lowe's name in the background and Early heard a muffled conversation as Lowe put his hand over the mouthpiece of his phone.

'I have to go, Early. Can you get up here and I can explain it all better face to face?'

'I don't know. I mean, I'll have to clear it with the sheriff.'

'Kapnick? Look, never mind clearing it first. I'll have my boss call him to sort it out.'

Early wasn't aware that Lowe knew Kapnick. So far as he was aware they had never met.

'How will I know exactly where you are?' Early asked.

'You'll know. Place is crawling with law enforcement. See you soon.'

The line went dead. Early called Shirley Lee and told her he was going to see the FBI. He did not elaborate when she asked what she was supposed to tell the sheriff.

The role of the FBI is not just the investigation of federal crimes, it also provides training and leadership to local law enforcement agencies. Three years ago Early had enrolled for a course in Boston that the FBI was running in conjunction with the Massachusetts State Police. Sheriff Kapnick had not authorised it when Early asked if the department would cover the cost so Early paid for it himself and took a week's leave of absence. He liked his job and wanted to perform it to the best of his abilities. He was not certain that Kappy shared that vision for his deputies.

Nick Lowe was the FBI special agent running the training course and he and Early had hit it off to the extent that they stayed in touch and met up for the occasional beer. Lowe was a career agent: graduating to the FBI Academy straight out of Michigan University ten years ago at age twenty-three. After twenty weeks of intense training at Quantico, he was officially a special agent. And he loved his job.

Early drove north on Highway 28, crossing onto mainland Massachusetts over the Bourne Bridge. The sky was clear today and the sun warm. Early wore sunglasses and perched his arm on his door, the window open and the wind ruffling his hair. He was not sure of the route to Sandy Pond Road, though it was only a short distance from the bridge. He followed the directions from the car's GPS, turning off the highway onto Bournedale Road and through Sacrifice Rock Woods. It was then a short drive north along Herring Pond Road to its intersection with Sandy Pond Road.

Early heard the helicopter hovering over the woods on his left as he neared the intersection. He leaned forward and looked up at the aircraft. The turn onto Sandy Pond Road was blocked by Plymouth police department cruisers with two uniformed officers standing behind them. Early rolled his patrol car to a stop short of the turn, pulled on his sheriff's department baseball cap and stepped out, nodding at the two men. He approached the first car, looking along the road and saw more cars parked along the side of the road, some of them plain FBI cars – 'Bucars' in the vernacular.

'Can I help you, buddy?' the taller of the two local officers asked.

Early did not care for the faint edge of condescension, but was used to it when coming into contact with officials from bigger forces.

'I'm here to speak to Special Agent Lowe,' Early told him. 'I'm guessing he's up the road there.'

Early lifted his chin in the direction of the parked cars. Above the woods, the helicopter rotated and shifted its position.

'You call ahead and tell him I'm here, I'm sure he'll ask you to let me through.'

'Hold on a second, deputy.'

The man stepped back from the car and turned his back to Early, keying the send button on the microphone of his radio.

Early looked at the other officer and smiled.

'Be a hot one today,' he said.

'Surely will.'

The taller man got the okay to allow Early through the roadblock. Both men got in their vehicles and moved them aside to allow Early access. Early said thanks and went back to his car, turning it onto Sandy Pond Road and driving slowly until the woods on his left opened out into a long driveway filled with more cars and law enforcement personnel.

Early drove past the driveway and parked. His phone rang as he got out of the car – it was Kapnick. Early saw Nick Lowe coming towards him from a modern looking house at the end of the driveway. Early held a finger up to Lowe, asking him to hold on while he answered the call from Kapnick.

'I got a call from the feds this morning,' Kapnick said to Early.

'Okay,' Early said.

'Some mess it seems they have.'

Early looked over Lowe's shoulder at the activity in and around the house. The front door was open and Early saw a number of what were obviously scenes of crime forensics staff moving inside the house. He counted two additional FBI agents dressed in blue raid jackets with 'FBI' in large yellow lettering on the back. They wore cargo pants under their jackets and stood directing the forensics team.

'I haven't been briefed yet,' he told Kapnick.

'Take your time.'

Early waited for his boss to say something else. He did not.

'You need me for anything, give me a call,' Early said.

Early put his phone back in the holder attached to his belt and smiled thinly at the FBI agent standing in front of him. Lowe was dressed in the same manner as his fellow agents. He shook Early's hand firmly. Lowe was not a large man, but he was wiry and strong in the mode of a boxer from the lower weight classes. His dark hair was conservatively short and neatly parted on the side. Sweat beaded his forehead and he wiped at it with the sleeve of his jacket.

'Good to see you, Bubba,' Lowe said, grinning.

Lowe had given call signs to all of the members of the training group from Boston. He admitted to Early one night that he had misjudged him; that he had initially made him for a slow-witted, meathead. But the name stuck with the other trainees. Early didn't mind it. It was the first time in his life that he had an actual nickname.

'This looks serious,' Early said.

Lowe looked back at the house and nodded.

'But you surely have enough people here to keep it under control.'

'So why did I ask you to come?'

'Yeah.'

'Follow me and I'll introduce you to the rest of the task force.'

Early frowned.

'I'm part of a task force?'

Lowe said yes and moved away from Early towards the house.

36

Early was surprised to find that one of the other agents was a woman. When he had seen them from the top of the driveway, he was sure that they were both men; based on their build and the way in which they moved. She was tall and broad shouldered for a woman and wore her hair short, with the sides and the back cropped close. When she turned to be introduced by Lowe, Early saw that she had delicate features: high cheekbones and a small nose. She wore no make-up and her skin glistened in the heat. Lowe introduced her as Agent Roberta Carlsson.

The other agent, Keller Parrish, was the same height as Carlsson at five-ten and had slightly longer fair hair. Early thought he looked like a California surfer dude who had grown up and gotten serious, but kept the same hairstyle.

'Where are the Staties?' Lowe asked Carlsson.

She turned and looked at the house.

'Inside, I think,' she said,

'Let's go find them.'

Early followed the three agents into the house. He saw broken glass from the window beside the front door. It smelled earthy inside the hall. Behind that was the metallic tang of cordite from gunfire. Early knew that people had died here.

They went right into a large living room that stretched from the front of the house to the back. There were two men in the room, both dressed in dark suits. One of the men was short and carrying a little too much weight. His suit jacket was draped over his left arm and sweat stains showed under his arms. He wiped at his shaved head with a handkerchief, his forearm displaying a fading military tattoo. A State Police detective badge was clipped to his belt beside a holstered revolver. Early made him for around fifty.

The other man was as tall as Early. His dark hair was thick and a fringe flopped over his forehead. He pushed it back with one hand. The sleeves of his white shirt were rolled neatly to his elbows and he looked unperturbed by the heat. He wore a nine-millimetre automatic on his belt and looked a good twenty years younger than his partner.

Lowe introduced the short detective as Scotty Pike. The other one was Travis McGee. The two detectives stared at Early, taking his measure. The FBI agents looked to Lowe to take the lead.

'This is what we know right now,' Lowe said. 'Around lunchtime yesterday two brothers, Marshall and Jimmy Cain, who have a passing acquaintance with law enforcement agencies, busted some heads at a bar outside of Boston. Some of it was caught on a camera that the owner has behind the bar. He set it up to keep an eye on his bar staff. You know, to see if they were dipping into the till.'

Lowe paused. Pike looked bored, turning his head and looking out the window into the back yard of the house.

'Local cops got a report on the fight around three in the afternoon. No one took much notice of it at the time. The victims were known to those cops.'

'Shithead on shithead violence is what we call it,' Pike said, turning back to Lowe.

Early stayed quiet, figuring that was his role right now. He didn't much care for Pike's cynicism. It seemed forced to Early, like Pike thought that was how seasoned cops were supposed to behave.

'Anyway,' Lowe went on, ignoring Pike, 'later, around six thirty, cops in Foxboro got a call reporting shots fired in a residential neighbourhood. They found two dead and signs that a third person, a teenage girl, might have been taken.'

'They found uneaten food from a local burger joint,' the female agent, Carlsson, said. 'One of the cops showed initiative and immediately asked for another car to go to the burger place to see if they had cameras that might have recorded something.'

'Right,' Lowe said. 'The cops that went to the burger place looked at the film from the cameras inside the place there and then.'

'That was smart,' Early added. 'I mean, not waiting till they got it back to the station.'

'Yeah, it was good work. No doubt.'

'They see film of the dead guy exchanging words with two guys eating at a table,' Carlsson went on. 'These two guys follow the other guy after he leaves.'

'The cops don't know it at the time,' Lowe said, 'but it's the brothers from the bar.'

Early wondered where this was going and what it had to do with events at this house.

'A state-wide alert goes out on the girl from the scene of the killings. Photo to all local agencies. Which brings us here.'

'You found the girl?' Early asked.

Lowe nodded, his mouth going tight. Early knew what it meant.

'Homeowner called nine-one-one in the early hours this morning. Something about a girl and men chasing her. At this point there's still no link been made between the attack at the bar and in Foxboro. A patrol car arrives here and finds the girl upstairs shot to death.'

'Along with a teenage boy and his father,' Carlsson added. 'Both dead.'

'Woman that made the nine-one-one call is still alive. She's in hospital right now. Bullet fractured her skull.'

'Same guys did this?' Early asked. 'I mean, that's some escalation from a bar fight.'

'We can't confirm it yet,' Lowe said, 'but we have them

positively identified from film at both the bar and the burger place.'

'You find the girl here and suddenly it looks like these boys went on a killing spree.'

'Correct,' Detective McGee said, speaking for the first time. 'We got the call and as soon as we identified the girl from the state-wide alert we called in these guys.'

He inclined his head towards the FBI agents.

Early took his cap off and rubbed at his head.

'Are you putting pictures of these boys out to local and state news agencies?' he asked.

Lowe shook his head. Early could tell from the faces of the state detectives that they did not agree with that decision.

'I don't want anyone approaching these guys but law enforcement,' Lowe said. 'The last thing we need is some yahoo with a gun re-enacting the OK Corral.'

'You said something about a task force?' Early said.

Lowe nodded.

'We need local knowledge on this.'

'Why am I here? I mean, you've got the state detectives. I don't see where I fit in.'

'Traffic camera on the Sagamore Bridge caught the brothers' car heading onto the Cape couple hours ago. I wanted someone I trusted.'

Early didn't know how to respond to the compliment. He put his cap back on and stuffed his hands into his trouser pockets.

'I'll do what I can to help,' he said.

37

Jimmy Cain locked the door of the restroom at the gas station and stared at his face in the mirror. His nose looked worse than it felt, and that was going some. His clothes were soaked in blood. He unbuttoned his shirt and slipped out of his jeans, dropping them onto the concrete floor. His body was leaner now than it used to be. Prison will do that to a man. But he worked at keeping in shape. His muscles were not large, but they were firm.

Jimmy filled the sink with hot water and rubbed the bar of cheap soap between his hands until the water foamed. He pulled a wad of paper from the dispenser on the wall, steeping the paper in the soapy water and gingerly washing his face. He took care to avoid his nose as much as possible. When he was done, he drained the sink, rinsed it out with more hot water and wiped his face with fresh paper. After that, he ran wet hands through his hair.

Someone knocked at the door.

'It's me,' Marshall said.

Jimmy unlocked the door. His brother handed him a bag with fresh clothes and a large sports bag. Marshall waited for his praise. Jimmy closed the door and locked it again.

The sports bag was big enough to hold the shotgun. There was a blue, a long-sleeved t-shirt and a cheap pair of canvas work trousers in the bag. Marshall had managed to get the right size so Jimmy pulled them on and examined himself in the mirror. He looked rough, but much better than before.

A line of blood ran from one nostril. He grabbed a piece of paper and wiped at it, snorting and spitting more blood into the sink. He ripped off a small piece of paper and gently pushed it into the nostril to stop the bleeding, wincing in pain as he did it.

Jimmy squinted in the bright sun outside. Marshall was leaning on the bonnet of the car with his face turned to the sky. For all the shit he had dragged them through, Jimmy thought that his brother looked none the worse for it.

'We need to get rid of the car,' Jimmy told Marshall.

His brother stepped away from the car.

'How do we get home?' he asked.

Marshall's face was blank.

'We're not going home, Marshall. We can't. Not after last night.'

'I guess,' he said. 'So where do we go?'

Something that looked like sadness passed across Marshall's face. But it was only momentary. Jimmy ignored the question and went to the trunk of the car, lifting it open. He put the sports bag on floor of the trunk and put the shotgun and the boxes of ammunition into the bag. He zipped it shut and lifted it out, slamming the trunk closed.

Jimmy looked at the cars passing on the road behind his brother. He felt oddly free. Like life had suddenly opened up in front of him.

'Where do you want to go?' Jimmy asked.

38

The first time that John Lustig saw his father cry was the day he came home from school at age eight and found him curled up on his bed, pulling the bed clothes to his chest and openly sobbing.

John Lustig had thrown his schoolbag onto the floor and slammed the front door, like he always did. He shouted 'Mom,' and waited. Usually she would come get him, hand him a can of Coke and pick up his bag, rolling her eyes because she had to tell him every day not to leave his bag there on the floor. This time, his mom did not appear.

John shouted for her again. When she didn't come, he went through the door from the hall to the living room expecting to find her in there listening to some music on her headphones. He knew that she liked to listen to old stuff like the Beatles when no one was around and figured maybe she had lost track of time. But she wasn't there.

She wasn't in the kitchen either so he went back to the hall and started up the stairs. That was when he started to hear the noise from his parents' room. He couldn't work out what it was to begin with.

One time the previous winter, when everyone was sent home from school early after the heating system broke, he'd heard some noise from up there. When he had shouted for his mom that day, she came down from the room looking all flustered. She took him into the kitchen to get a drink. He heard the front door close a couple minutes later. When he asked his mom if someone else had been in the house, she laughed weirdly and waved his question away.

But the noise this time was different. He pushed the door of his parents' room open and went inside. He saw his father. Then he saw the mess in the rest of the room: a picture frame smashed on the floor, a crack in the glass of the window and clothes all over the place.

Theodore Lustig stared at his son but made no move to get up from his position on the bed. John watched him for a while and eventually the man stopped crying. He sat up and wiped at his eyes with his hands. John waited.

He had always been an unemotional child. Seeing his father like this did not upset him in a conventional way. His primary feeling was one of disgust. Men were not supposed to cry; that was something women did. Or girls. Sure, John had cried before but that was because he was a little kid. It was okay for kids to cry when their dad hit them across the back of their bare legs or their butt with a leather belt. But now, here was this big tough guy and he was acting like a girl.

'C'mere, John,' his father said, holding his arms out like he wanted a hug.

John leaned against the wall. He knew that by doing so he was risking the belt, but for some reason the thought of hugging his father right now felt like it would be worse than getting whacked.

'John,' his father said, his chin quivering.

'Where's mom?'

Theodore Lustig dropped his hands and stared at his son. He seemed empty in that moment, a Halloween pumpkin scraped of its guts.

'She left us.'

John was not hugely surprised by this news. His parents had been fighting more and more over the last few months. It had started, he seemed to recall, after that day the school got closed and he came home early.

His mom was never an overly tactile woman. She rarely

hugged John though she always kissed his cheek and patted him on the head when she sent him out to meet the school bus.

He only saw his mom two times after that day. Once when she came to the house to pick up some boxes of stuff that his dad had filled and another time in court when the divorce got finalised. Both times she never made eye contact with him.

After the divorce, his father threw himself into his work and John pretty much had to fend for himself with a series of part-time nannies and housekeepers. His father complained to him all the time about how much all of that cost. They went on one holiday every year in June which his father spent mainly drinking beer and sleeping.

John got the fuck out of that house when he was seventeen, busting his ass as a waiter to earn enough to cover the rent for a shit-hole apartment. He learned the restaurant trade from the bottom up. Did it all by himself.

He didn't much think of those times any more and was surprised that those memories would surface now. After calling Kate and Joe last night, Lustig had gotten busy. He had set about cleaning the apartment. It wasn't looking too bad now, though the smell of the burned food still lingered.

Lustig sat in the living room and, for what seemed like the hundredth time, checked to make sure that his gun was loaded and the safety engaged.

Got to be prepared.

Got to be careful.

When he was satisfied, he placed the gun carefully on the table beside his chair. He recalled that this used to be his apartment – before he married Kate. Now it was theirs. He had two choices, he realised – get her back here or get rid of the place. The logic of any other option did not strike him as remotely acceptable.

He had thought about their relationship long and hard over the course of the night, while he cleaned.

They met at his restaurant two years ago. He had not had a single relationship that had lasted for more than three months his whole life. He got bored of the company of women quickly and when the excitement of a having new body to explore wore off he got out of there.

He wasn't sure why Kate had affected him the way she had. First time they met was when she sent her steak back to the kitchen for the second time because it was overcooked. Lustig took pride in customer satisfaction and so had gone out to deal with her complaint personally. She was with a group of attorneys from her law firm, celebrating some big case they had settled. He didn't care much for attorneys. He had kept clear of them since his parent's divorce except when he could not avoid using them for business.

Kate was so sweet that night, telling him not to worry about the food and thanks so much for caring enough to speak to her. She started to come into the restaurant a lot he noticed. He made a point of visiting her table and making sure her food was perfect. He told his chefs not to screw up her orders.

She hung around the restaurant late one night, sipping her wine slowly as the tables around her emptied. They wound up back here at the apartment. He never seemed to tire of her the way he did other women. He didn't know if it was love he felt, but he enjoyed her company. The place felt too big when she wasn't there.

Kate's number glowed on the screen of his phone. He looked at it for a moment and answered the call.

Be nice and she'll talk to you, he thought. *Play it like that first time.*

'Hey, Kate,' he said, unconsciously laying his free hand on top of the gun beside him.

39

Kate Foley had woken late to the sound of her father whistling as he worked in the back yard. It seemed to Kate that he spent more time in the garden than anywhere else since he retired. She felt better for having slept there; felt safe.

She got up and showered before calling her office and explaining that she needed a couple of days away from her desk to deal with family matters. She was on the verge of partnership at the firm and well liked. She knew that nobody would have any problem with her taking the time. After reassuring her boss that everything was okay and that he did not need to worry about her she ended the call and dressed in a pair of old chinos and a sleeveless blouse. Her parents had maintained a room for her since she left home with a small supply of clothes. Kate had often asked why they did that, never getting what she thought was a satisfactory explanation.

Joe Foley was on his knees tending to his flowers when Kate came out from the kitchen and handed him a glass of water. He took an old baseball cap off his head and wiped a sleeve across his forehead. The sleeve darkened immediately from the sweat it absorbed. Joe said thanks and drank half the water in one go. Kate took a sip of coffee from her mug and ran a hand through her father's hair, lifting it off of his forehead.

'Things don't look nearly so bad in the morning,' Kate said, smiling.

Joe took a smaller drink of the water and rubbed dirt from his hands onto the thighs of his jeans.

'Sun pushes the dark away for a while, that's for sure,' he said.

Kate frowned at him.

'You trying to spoil my good mood, Dad? Cause it won't work.'

It was hard for Joe to see past the damage to his daughter's face and he told her so. Kate put a hand gently to the bruising.

'I'm trying to forget,' she told her father.

'Maybe you shouldn't. Maybe the best thing is to do something about it while what he did to you can be seen.'

Kate sighed. So much for her good mood. She looked past the garden to the beach where two young boys were running along the water's edge, trying to avoid the waves as the tide came in. A black Labrador dog ran ahead of them, not caring about getting wet as it splashed into the water to retrieve a piece of driftwood.

'Where's mom?'

'Gone into town, she said. Probably meeting one of her friends. She doesn't tell me much.'

Kate wasn't sure if he was joking. She had always thought that her parents had a good marriage, never recalling any major fights or walk-outs.

Joe Foley stood and finished the last of the water. He handed the empty glass to Kate and thanked her.

'I think maybe I should try to speak to John,' Kate said.

Her father stuffed his hands into the pockets of his jeans.

'Do you think that's a good idea? I mean, after the way he was on the phone last night. He didn't sound in a good way to me.'

Kate nodded.

'I know, but…'

'What?'

'It's not going to get better by me doing nothing, is it? We're still married and there are things we need to sort out.'

'So the marriage is over?'

'As far as I'm concerned, it is.'

Joe nodded.

'That's a good start. But I don't think you should see him alone. Not until you work out what's really going on inside his head.'

'If I meet him somewhere open and public it'll be okay.'

Joe reached out and held his daughter's free hand, pulling her towards him.

'You're my only child, Kate. And I love you more than you can know.'

'I know that, Dad.'

'For my peace of mind, don't see that man on your own. You can't trust him. And I don't know that I could go on if I lost you like that.'

Kate squeezed her father's hand.

'You won't. John may not be husband of the year, but he's not truly bad. I can't believe that I would marry a man like that.'

Joe Foley put his hat back on and took some time getting it in just the right position. The cloth was stained with sweat where it met the peak of the cap.

'One thing I learned as a lawyer, Kate,' he started.

'Just the one thing?' Kate smiled.

Joe ignored her gentle ribbing.

'You can never know a person. I mean, not really. Believe me.'

Kate did not respond, watching her father's eyes closely.

'I don't like the way John sounded last night.'

Kate held her coffee cup to the side and hugged her father with her other arm. He held on until she pulled away.

'I'll speak to him on the phone first,' she said. 'Okay? See how he sounds.'

'You'll still take someone with you if you go to see him, right?'

'Are you volunteering?' Kate smiled, trying to make light of it.

'You don't need an old fart like me. I mean, what use would I be if things got out of hand?'

Kate knew someone that would be able to help. But having Early Simms at a meeting with her husband was not a good idea. She could see her father reading her eyes.

'Let me know if you decide to go see him' Joe said, 'and I'll make sure that you have company.'

Kate leaned in and kissed her father on the cheek.

'You know people, Dad. Is that it?'

She smiled again and turned away from him.

Joe watched his daughter walk back to the house, lifting a hand to shield his eyes from the sun.

40

'How are you today, John?' Kate asked her husband.

'I'm okay, you know. Just…'

He didn't finish the sentence. His voice sounded normal again – not like last night. She was glad.

'Listen, John. I'm going to take a few days away from the city.'

'Sure. Clear your head. That's a good idea.'

'You assaulted me, John.'

He was quiet.

'You understand that?' Kate asked. 'I mean, do you accept that's what happened?'

'Yes.'

'It's good that you can admit it.'

'I assaulted you.'

His voice started to move up in pitch.

'I'm not coming back to the apartment. I can't live with you any more. Not after what happened. I won't be a victim, John. I've seen too much of it in my work.'

'You want a divorce? Is that what you're saying, Kate?'

Kate thought that his voice had normalised again – if that was even a word that could be applied to the man any more.

'I'm not saying that.'

'It sure sounds like it. I mean, how do we stay married but never live together?'

'It's too soon for us to talk about all of that. I just wanted to make sure you were okay and that you understood how serious this is, you know.'

'I'm okay and this is serious. I get it.'

'I haven't called the police, John. I could have, but I didn't.'

'Thank you.'

'That didn't sound sincere.'

'What the fuck do you want me to say?' he screamed at her.

Kate pulled the phone from her ear. She stared at it, not sure how to react.

'Sorry,' she heard him say. 'Sorry. Sorry.'

'I think it's best if we don't speak for a few days,' Kate said, bringing the phone back to her ear. 'Let things cool down, you know.'

'Cool down. Sure.'

'Bye, John.'

She ended the call without waiting for a reply, turning to go back to her room. She saw her father standing inside the open door to the yard.

'I guess you won't be meeting him right now?' Joe Foley asked.

'You spying on me, Dad?'

'Maybe.'

'I think I'd like it if you keep on doing that. Just for a bit, you know.'

Kate smiled uncertainly. Joe Foley nodded.

41

The two state police detectives, Pike and McGee, were out in the back yard of the Applegate house. Early was in the living room, watching them through the window. He was alone, waiting for Lowe to finish directing the forensic team out front. Lowe wanted the grounds of the house searched from the doorstep to the boundary and did not trust anyone else to get that message over. Early thought that Lowe was an intense man who would not be able to spend a whole career dealing with criminals in a frontline role. That level of stress would be too much for a man of Lowe's disposition. Early did not think less of his friend for that. He knew that dealing with evil of the kind that had been visited upon this family on a regular basis would likely force him out of law enforcement too.

There were photos of the family in this room. The parents looked strong and confident in their lives. The boy did not appear to share that attitude, if a series of photographs could ever fully capture the essence of a person. He looked…overshadowed.

The other FBI agents were out in the hall. Early heard the woman, Carlsson, talking to someone though he could not make out what was being said. He wondered about the effort that was going into the investigation here at the house. They appeared to have identified the killers and knew where they had been a few short hours ago. It seemed to Early as if this case was not going to be won or lost on forensics, but rather on who had the ability to hold their nerve when the only options were dying or killing. He had never faced such a situation.

'You got any thoughts, Bubba?' Lowe asked from the doorway.

Early looked up and shrugged.

'Come on,' Lowe said. 'I know that you always have something to contribute. I mean, it's one of the reasons I asked my boss to let me call you in on this. I've wanted to see what you might be like on a real case since that classroom in Boston.'

Early walked to the window facing the driveway.

'All these people look real busy,' Early said. 'I mean, lots of striding around with purpose.'

Lowe frowned and leaned on the doorframe but said nothing.

'But the fact is you have two men out there somewhere who have graduated in the space of a day from a bar fight to a massacre. And you know who they are.'

'We have a strong lead on their identity.'

Early turned to look at Lowe.

'I'm not in the Bureau chain of command, Nick. So, you know, you don't have to talk to me like that.'

Lowe nodded once.

'Where are you going with this?' he asked.

Early sat back against the window ledge, resting his hands on his thighs. The sun felt warm on his back through the glass. He caught a whiff again of the smells from deeper within the house.

'This is a manhunt, plain and simple. All this stuff…'

Early nodded at the scene outside the window.

'Well, I mean, it's just folk doing their job. Processing stuff because the rulebook says they have to.'

'When we catch these men, it will all be necessary process. We need it to get the right result.'

Early wasn't sure that he was being clear in expressing his views.

'Show me where they were killed,' he told Lowe.

'You want to see that?'

'No. But *want* doesn't really come into it now, does it?'

The smells got stronger out in the hall and grew in intensity as they climbed the stairs towards the bedrooms.

'The ME took the bodies already,' Lowe told Early. 'And the forensics are pretty much done up here.'

There was one other person on the second floor; a photographer walked slowly along the hallway taking shots of blood traces on the walls and floor. He stopped and waited for Lowe and Early to walk past, heading for the master suite.

The door of the room was half open. Early waited for Lowe to enter the room and followed him inside.

Lowe walked to the closet on the right-hand side of the room. He raised his arm and pointed to the opposite wall.

'Found the wife over there. Thought she was dead to begin with. Amount of blood, you know.'

Early nodded.

'They got her loaded into an ambulance fast as they could and over to the hospital in Plymouth. They have a specialist head trauma unit over there.'

'She going to make it?'

'Last we heard. Lucky woman.'

Early wondered if she would count herself lucky once she came to the realisation that the people she loved most in this world were both dead. He did not voice that thought to Lowe.

Lowe pointed at the broken window with his chin.

'Far as we can tell the husband was shot in here and fell out into the yard. The son was on the floor in front of the window.'

A huge amount of blood had soaked into the carpet by the window. It was congealing and turning dark. Early blinked as the sun reflected in the pool outside and knifed into the room.

'Girl was here,' Lowe said looking down at the corner of the room where Brianna Chalk had died.

Lowe started at the wall where pieces of Brianna's skin clung to the wall, stuck there by her own blood.

'You have any idea how it went down?' Early asked Lowe.

Lowe shook his head.

'Not really. We recovered an unregistered handgun. We're missing a shotgun and Sig that the husband owned.'

'He was into guns?'

'Ran a security company. Successful by all accounts. I mean, from what we can tell he operated in Afghanistan. A serious individual.'

'He let two amateurs do this to his family.'

'Yes.'

Early stood and put his cap on.

'We better put a rush on finding these guys.'

42

In her dream, Missy Applegate is swimming in the pool in her yard. She's moving fast through the water with a powerful backstroke. Her eyes are open and she's staring up at a brilliant, cobalt blue sky.

All that Missy can hear is the sound of water rushing past her ears and her breath, rhythmic and deep.

She knows how many strokes it takes for her to complete a length of the pool and she slows, anticipating the turn. But this time the pool does not end. She wants to stop and turn to see what's wrong. But, like all the best (worst) nightmares, she can't will her body to do anything. So she keeps on swimming.

And swimming.

Missy starts to feel tired, her muscles aching and her breath becoming laboured. She doesn't know how long she's been going, but the bright blue above her is changing. A red/orange glow fills her field of vision.

She turns her head and sees Hank standing at the window of their bedroom. He's smiling at her. Missy smiles too, relieved that everything is alright after all.

Then she sees that Hank is unmoving, frozen in place.

Someone is in the room with Hank. Missy can see a dark figure moving around in there. She wants to stop and scream at Hank to turn around.

She keeps on swimming but the world around her does not move. She is stuck in place, swimming as fast as she can but unable to make any progress.

The figure behind Hank comes into sharper focus. It is her son, Jordan. He's smiling too. But that does not comfort Missy.

Jordan looks the way he did on his fifth birthday. His hair is tousled and his eyes are heavy from sleep. He's wearing his favourite PJs, the ones with a cowhide pattern and a hood with cow ears. She remembers him coming into her bedroom in those jammies and pushing at her back to wake her.

'Moooove over,' he says in his little boy voice.

Missy remembered laughing till she cried at his joke; this little boy that she loved so much.

Five-year-old Jordan in his cow PJs stops behind Hank and raises a gun to point it at the back of his father's head.

Missy opens her mouth to scream. Water rushes into her lungs instead of air. She chokes and gags on the water as the world around her fades to black.

43

Missy woke up. She turned her head and a shard of pain jagged into her brain. She hissed in a breath and held her head still, waiting for the pain to pass.

She was in a hospital – that much she knew. The fear and frustration she felt in her dream lingered even in the light of the sun that streamed into her room. Her thoughts would not coalesce, though a feeling of deep dread started to wash over her.

She remembered the little boy in the cow jammies.

And the strong, handsome man that she married.

The door to her room opened and she saw a uniformed police officer sitting on a chair in the corridor outside. A male nurse, no older than twenty-five, came into the room and smiled at her. Missy did not react.

The nurse walked to her bed and looked down at her.

'How are you feeling?'

Missy looked up at him. His smile faded.

'Where's my boy?' she asked, her voice no more than a whisper. 'Where's Jordan?'

Missy was aware of the cop turning his head at the sound of her voice.

The nurse put on his best concerned face and shook his head.

'Just sleep for now, okay.'

The cop stood and came into the room, leaning against the wall just inside the door.

'Where is my son?' Missy said.

The nurse turned to look at the cop. He shrugged his shoulders: it's up to you.

'I'm so sorry,' the nurse said, turning back to Missy.

She tried to sit up but pain blasted her down. She gritted her teeth and waited for it to pass. Her forehead felt hot and sticky.

'Tell me,' Missy said, her voice as strong as she could make it.

'Your son died.'

She closed her eyes.

'And Hank?'

The cop stepped forward.

'I'm afraid he didn't make it, Ma'am.'

Missy tried to open her eyes but all she saw was black, fading into unconsciousness.

This time there was no dream.

Only darkness.

44

Nick Lowe sat in the passenger seat of Early's department cruiser as they passed over the Bourne Bridge and onto Cape Cod. Lowe pushed his sunglasses up on his nose. They had not spoken much since leaving the Applegate house.

'So what's your story, Bubba?' Lowe asked. 'You going to wait till Kapnick's gone and then take that sheriff's badge?'

'That's the second time you've spoken about my boss as if you know him. Far as I know, the two of you never met.'

Early didn't look at Lowe, keeping his eyes on the road ahead.

'You don't miss much,' Lowe said.

Early did not respond.

Lowe took his sunglasses off and wiped at them with his shirt, holding them up against the light to check when he was done. Early waited.

'You're right,' Lowe said, rubbing at his glasses again, 'I never met him.'

'You telling me to mind my own business, special agent?'

'I'm telling you I never met the man. And you're ignoring my question.'

'I don't think that far ahead,' Early said, slowing to turn left and waiting for a pick-up truck to pass.

Lowe put his glasses back on and smiled.

'I got to give it to you,' he told Early. 'You got this whole small-town deputy thing down pat. I mean, it's almost believable.'

Early couldn't help but smile, glad that the mood had lightened for a moment.

'You forget that I know how good you are,' Lowe said. 'You were the smartest guy in the room when I taught that course. And I include myself in that assessment.'

'I'm happy doing what I'm doing.'

'I believe that. I just don't buy that you'll always be happy doing it.'

'I guess I'll retire some day.'

Lowe laughed.

'Man, do you have it down pat.'

The parked outside the sheriff's department building. Early felt the heat of the sun on his head when he stepped out of the car. He put his cap on and led Lowe past Shirley Lee and into the deputies' office. Frank Wood was there alone. Early introduced him to Lowe. Wood looked genuinely impressed to be meeting a bona fide federal agent.

Early told Lowe to wait while he checked in with the sheriff.

'He ain't in,' Wood said.

'Where did he go?'

'Didn't say. Told me to hold the fort a half hour ago and left.'

Early rubbed his chin and looked at Lowe. The agent remained impassive.

'Did we get any alerts in yesterday or this morning?' Early asked Wood.

'Yeah…'

Wood pulled at the pile of papers on his desk but did not find what he was looking for. He got up and went to Randolph Jones's desk. He grabbed at two sheets and brandished them at Early like a proud child with his first school report. Early took them from Wood and read the first alert on Brianna Chalk and the murder of her parents. The second one, dated this morning, named Marshall and James Cain as suspects in multiple homicides and gave details of the car. There were grainy colour photographs of both men. Jimmy's was from a law enforcement facility – Early recognised the institutional quality immediately.

'What's up?' Wood asked Lowe. 'I mean, anything we can help with?'

For all of his bravado, Early did not think that Frank Wood was someone that he would want by his side in the event that he came face to face with the Cain brothers.

'Not just yet, Frank.'

Early went out into the hall, folding the sheet with the photos and putting it in his breast pocket. Lowe followed him out of the deputies' room.

'What now?' Early asked.

'That alert is out there. Matter of time before someone finds those boys.'

Early wasn't so sure.

'I could use a cup of coffee,' Lowe said. 'A real one. Not some two-day old crap from a police station.'

'I know a place,' Early said.

45

They went across the street to Kennedy's. Pat Kennedy turned when he heard the door open. He smiled at Early and set two cups on the counter, filling them with coffee. There were two young men at a table in back eating eggs and bacon.

'Morning, Pat,' Early said, nodding at the man and putting his cap on the counter beside his cup.

Kennedy nodded in return.

'Who's your friend?' he asked.

'This is Nick.'

Kennedy wiped his right hand on an apron tied around his waist and extended it to shake Lowe's hand.

'You a cop?' Kennedy asked Lowe.

'Federal agent.'

'You want milk, Federal Agent Nick?'

Lowe smiled and shook his head.

'Black is fine, thanks.'

'Anything to eat?'

Early said no. Kennedy took the coffee pot and went to the table at the back to refresh the cups of his only other customers. Early looked at his watch. It was not far off noon.

Lowe took a drink and scanned the photos on the wall behind the counter. He set the cup down.

'That you over there?'

Early said that it was.

'Were you any good?'

'I was okay.'

Early's phone rang. He unhooked it from his belt, got off the stool and walked to the front of the diner, looking out the window onto Main Street.

'Early, it's Kate.'

'Hey. How are you today? How's the face?'

'As you would expect.'

'I guess that was a pretty stupid question.'

'I'm going to stay at my parents' place for a few days.'

'What about your office? I mean, are they okay with that?'

'It's fine.'

Early liked hearing her voice. When they had been together back in school and he dropped her off at home she always told him to call her when he got home. It was usually a conversation that lasted no more than a few seconds: that's me home; good, see you at school tomorrow; love you, bye.

Early had always thought she wanted to make sure he made it back safe. Now, he wondered if it was really just to hear his voice one more time before she went to bed. Hearing her again now after last night, he understood.

'It's good to hear from you,' he said, wincing at the clumsiness of it.

'Is it?'

'Yes.'

'I mean, after what you said last night I wasn't sure…'

Early looked back at Lowe. He was engaged in what looked like a serious conversation with Pat Kennedy. Early frowned as Kennedy pointed at Early's photo on the wall.

'Listen, Kate, I have to go now. I'm in the middle of something.'

'Sure.'

He realised how abrupt he must have sounded.

'Sorry. I didn't mean to…'

'No, it's okay. I understand.'

'Can I call you later? After work, I mean.'

'I'd like that.'

'Take care of yourself, Kate.'

He walked back to Lowe and took a gulp of coffee, still standing. Pat Kennedy took a step back from the counter.

'We got work to do,' Early said to Lowe.

Lowe stared at Early before taking out his billfold and placing five dollars on the counter.

'Thanks,' he said to Kennedy.

'The old fella was telling me about your dad,' Lowe said as they walked out of the diner. 'Sorry to hear about that.'

'Was that all?'

Lowe stopped and put a hand on Early's arm.

'What's eating you? I mean, the way you pulled me out of there was a little rude.'

Early stopped at the edge of the sidewalk and turned to Lowe.

'I don't like people talking about my business.'

Lowe held his hands up.

'From what I can tell I think that old man cares about your dad, Early. And about you.'

Early put his hands in his trouser pockets and looked inside the diner. Pat Kennedy turned his head quickly as if he had been watching them and was ashamed to have been caught.

'Small towns are like that,' Lowe said. 'Everyone knows everyone.'

Early didn't know what to say. He left Lowe on the sidewalk and walked briskly across the street to the office.

46

Henry Kapnick was an only child and lost both parents in the space of nine months a few years ago. It happened liked that sometimes when people have been married for a long time; the survivor gives up and passes on shortly after the death of his or her partner. In Kapnick's case, his dad had died first; suffering a massive heart attack sitting on the couch watching the Super Bowl.

Kapnick had not been close to his parents for a long time. He saw them infrequently on birthdays and major holidays. He had never married and lived alone, apparently content with his own company. After his dad died, he had visited his mother more often and had seen the rapid deterioration in her physical condition. She rarely went out and ate little. It was almost as if she wanted to die. He had no time or sympathy for that kind of attitude. It was a minor relief when she died.

He had drifted apart from his dad after refusing to follow him into the fishing industry. He had worked with his dad on a couple of different boats before he was twenty and hated it. The sea was an inherently dangerous and unpredictable beast. It turned out that Henry Kapnick preferred the rigour and routine of life in uniform where chaos could be more readily reined in; or dealt out.

It also helped that drug dealers were willing to pay cops large amounts of cash to protect their business. And so far Kapnick had not been required to put himself seriously in harm's way. The altercation with Manu Polite was the first time that he had to strong-arm anyone. Kapnick had never had any trouble taking the stick to someone. He liked the sense of protection that the badge gave him.

Polite's problem was that he had questioned Kapnick's approach to skimming a tiny amount off the top. Polite said he wanted to keep his kneecaps intact. Kapnick hoped that the minor beating and a short stay at the County facility was enough to keep the man in line. Polite wasn't too smart, but he worked hard. And he was a man that was willing to take a lick now and then.

Polite came out of the main jail entrance and raised a hand to shield his eyes from the sun. He saw Kapnick sitting in a cruiser parked in one of the spaces usually reserved for the corrections officers. Kapnick opened his door and got out of the car, leaning on the open door and motioning for Polite to come to him. Polite dropped his hand and squinted at Kapnick.

'I thought maybe you would want a ride,' Kapnick said.

Polite looked back to the jail entrance as if he might find some help there.

'Come on, Manu. Let's you and me make up.'

Henry Kapnick was the first cop that Manu Polite had ever truly hated. He had locked horns with many law enforcement agencies in his forty-one years, but never got into it physically with any one of them. He knew that there was only ever one winner in that game and while he was not an educated man, he was not stupid. When Kapnick started on him that night it took all of Polite's resolve not to tear the man's head from his shoulders. Kapnick was a classic police bully and Polite had seen, and dealt with, many of them.

Polite walked to the front of the car, aware that he had to show some deference to Kapnick.

'I took it and I didn't tell no one,' Polite said. 'Ain't that enough.'

'Hey, Manu. You got it all wrong. I'm here to mend

fences. I don't have any problem with you.'

'What if I don't want to do it no more?'

Kapnick pushed his cap back on his head and sucked air in through his teeth.

'Come on. You know that's not how it works. I mean, you're in until I say you're not.'

'I don't got a say in it?'

Kapnick shook his head.

'Get in the fucking car, Manu.'

Polite had to listen to Kapnick's bullshit all the way back to town. About how he was real sorry about what happened between them, but that Polite knew that he had to do it.

'I mean, the chain of command is important, Manu. Got to maintain discipline, you know.'

Polite wondered if that's what Kapnick would say when staring down the barrel of a shotgun aimed at his face. He guessed that's what would happen if the men in Miami ever found out about Kapnick's sideline at their expense. Trouble was, Polite knew he'd fare no better. So he had to take whatever shit Kapnick dealt out.

They pulled up outside Manu's apartment block – a dingy two-storey affair beside a gas station at the northern boundary of Blackwater. Kapnick got out the car with Polite and followed him up the stairs and along the balcony to Polite's place. The smell of spilled gasoline fumes was strong in Polite's nostrils.

The apartment was a single room with a kitchenette in the corner and a door leading to the bathroom. The place was as Polite had left it, in need of a coat of paint but otherwise neat and tidy. He was a man that could not live any other way.

Kapnick let Polite open the door and walk in ahead of him. Kapnick closed the door, pulled his handgun and drew it hard across the back of Polite's head. Polite grunted and fell to his knees. He threw a hand out and grabbed the corner of his bed to prevent himself from going face first into the floor. He reached back with his other hand and clamped it over the wound on his head, blood starting to seep through his fingers. His head felt thick and darkness encroached at the edges of his vision. He vomited onto the floor.

'Look at the mess you made,' Kapnick said, shaking his head.

He kneeled beside Polite and pressed the muzzle of his gun hard into Polite's ear. Polite's head swirled and buzzed. He put a hand on the floor to steady himself. Kapnick reached around with his free hand and grabbed the other side of Polite's head, pressing the gun harder into his ear. Polite looked sideways at him, making no move to resist.

'I see it in your eyes, man,' Kapnick said. 'You want to hurt me, don't you?'

Polite tried to shake his head.

'Don't you fucking move or I'll pull the trigger.'

'I ain't moved.'

Kapnick held his position for a moment and then stood, training his gun on the top of Polite's head.

'We understand each other?' Kapnick asked.

Polite frowned, feeling blood trickle down his neck and under the collar of his shirt. His head started to clear of the fuzziness.

'I make the decisions and you do as you're told. That's the only way it works. We're in it together, you understand.'

Polite nodded. He was about done getting his ass kicked by this man but now was not the time to do anything about.

'I don't like the look in your eyes,' Kapnick said.

He kicked Polite on the side of the face with the point of his boot. Polite went over onto his side, his eyelids fluttering as unconsciousness took him.

Kapnick pointed his gun at the prone man's head. A dog barked outside as a car pulled into the gas station. Kapnick had never killed a man. He sometimes wondered how it would make him feel. He looked at Polite's bed and at the pillows neatly tucked under the bed clothes. He didn't know if using a pillow would mute the sound of the shot the way it seemed to do in the movies. It would certainly protect him from the blood spatter.

Kapnick holstered his gun and prodded Polite with his foot. There was no movement and he wondered if the combination of blows to the head had been too much. He hunkered down and felt Polite's wrist for a pulse. He was alive.

'I might have to kill you yet,' he told Polite.

Kapnick left the apartment with thoughts of a killing still on his mind.

47

Jimmy Cain liked the look of the motel that he saw out of the bus window. It was a mile or so from the centre of Hyannis, where Main Street turned into East Main Street. From what he could see, it backed onto woods leading to a residential neighbourhood. Jimmy was exhausted and wanted somewhere to hole up for a few days to get his head straight. This place looked as good as any. He nudged his older brother awake and pressed the call button telling the driver that he wanted off at the next stop.

The bus slowed and Jimmy stood in the aisle, steadying himself and reaching up to the shelf above his seat to get the sports bag with the shotgun in it. Jimmy figured it would be best if he took the shotgun and left Marshall with the handgun. Marshall had insisted, against Jimmy's judgement, in keeping the handgun stuffed into his jeans. Jimmy felt that it was too risky, but given Marshall's behaviour of the last twenty-four hours he wasn't about to get into a fight with him. Marshall sat with the gun covered by his shirt and his hand resting on top of it.

'We're getting off here, Marshall. Let's go.'

Marshall looked up at him, blinking sleep from his eyes.

'Where are we?'

'Hyannis.'

Marshall looked out the window as the bus slowed and pulled to the side of the road.

'I never been to Hyannis,' he said,

'Me neither, big brother.'

When they had been young, and after Marshall's accident, holidays for the Cain family were pretty much the same as any other day, except that the boys did not go to school. Money was always tight. There wasn't much left after their mother had drunk herself to sleep. So the boys looked after themselves. Sometimes they cooked beans and eggs at home while their mother snored on the couch in front of the TV. When they ran out of food they survived on water from the faucet supplemented by the occasional Coke they stole. If they were really lucky, a friend's mom would make them a sandwich or the old couple down the hall asked them in and fed them soup.

'How's your mom today?' the old lady would ask.

Jimmy usually shrugged and said she wasn't feeling well. He saw the looks that the old couple exchanged. He knew his mother was a drunk. There was nothing he could do about it.

'You looking after your brother, Jim?' the man asked.

He always shortened their names like that: Jim and Marsh. No one else called them by those names. Jimmy kind of liked it.

'Yes, sir.'

The old man died one summer and the lady moved away to stay with her family. She came to see Jimmy the day she left. Jimmy remembered that she looked different. She was thinner and her eyes no longer seemed to hold the light he used to see there.

She gave him a candy bar while her daughter hovered out in the hall with her bags. Jimmy's mom was out and Marshall was sleeping.

'You're the man of the house, Jimmy,' she told him, resting a hand on the top of his head.

He nodded.

'You have to look out for your brother.'

That was the last thing that she said to him. She kissed him on the cheek. He remembered that her lips felt thin and dry and that she smelled of talcum powder and cinnamon.

She never said anything about his mother, as if she did not exist, which was mostly true so far as Jimmy was concerned.

He never heard about the old lady again. He knew that she must have died but took comfort from the fact that he never had to hear anyone say it.

Jimmy paid cash for a room for three days. He told Marshall to wait outside the main office of the motel and to watch the bag. The female clerk couldn't help but stare at Jimmy's battered face. She wasn't any older than twenty. Jimmy figured she was a college student taking a shit job like this to make some money over summer break. Jimmy got tired of her stare.

'Something bothering you?' he asked as she gave him his change.

Her face blanched red. She pointed at his face.

'You got a…'

Jimmy wiped below his nose. His hand came away crusted with flakes of dried blood. The girl reached under the counter and handed him a tissue. He said thanks and tried to smile.

'What happened?' she asked.

Jimmy glanced at his brother through the glass doors to make sure he had not wandered off. He caught Marshall looking at the girl. He averted his eyes quickly when Jimmy turned round. Notwithstanding the bond he had with Marshall, Jimmy was concerned about his brother's attitude to women. It was his fault the Chalk girl had gotten away in the first place and did not need another problem here now.

'I got hit in the face with a baseball,' Jimmy told the girl, pointing at his nose. 'Stupid, huh? Playing ball at my age.'

The girl's eyes went down to his torso.

'I dunno,' she said. 'You look in good shape.'

'Yeah?' Jimmy patted his flat stomach. 'For a guy my age.'

The girl said he looked better than half the guys her age

and handed him the key to their room. Jimmy wasn't sure if she was flirting with him.

The room was on the first floor and face out into the courtyard, which was what Jimmy had asked for. He wanted to be able to see into the courtyard, better to know trouble was coming if the cops showed.

Marshall sat on his bed and flipped through TV channels while Jimmy went for a shower. It felt good to have a proper wash. He had felt grimy all day. He towelled dry and went into the main part of the room. Marshall was watching a movie Jimmy had not seen, some superhero thing.

Jimmy closed the blinds and turned the air conditioning down low. It rattled as if it might cut off altogether but kept going. He dropped his towel on the floor and climbed into bed naked. He was asleep in less than a minute.

48

It was dusk when Jimmy Cain woke. His mouth felt dry and his skin rough from where he had scrubbed himself clean in the shower. The air was cool and goose bumps rose on his skin when he sat up and the bed clothes dropped from his torso. He rubbed at his eyes and stretched his hands above his head, his shoulder joints popping as he did so.

The TV was on with the volume turned down low. An advertisement for a pick-up truck was on the channel – trying to sell more and more horsepower to city dwellers with small dicks.

Marshall was not in the room, though the top sheet was missing from his bed and the impression of his body could still be seen on the mattress. Jimmy swung his legs out of the bed and pulled on his underwear and trousers. He said Marshall's name, though he was not sure why. He could see the whole room. There was no sound from the bathroom and no light showing under the door. He remembered Marshall staring at the girl from reception and something dark fluttered in Jimmy's stomach.

He went to the front door and pulled it open, looking both ways along the row of rooms and out into the courtyard. He did not see Marshall. Across the road from the motel the sign for a McDonalds restaurant flickered to life in the gloom. Jimmy could not recall noticing the restaurant when they had arrived. A door opened to Jimmy's left. He closed the door and stood with his back against it. It felt too cold in the room.

He saw Marshall's handgun sitting on the TV unit. The bag with his shotgun was on the floor at the base of the unit. He went to the bag and was relieved to see the weapon still there.

Jimmy opened the bathroom door and switched the light on. Marshall blinked against the light from the bare bulb and pulled the top sheet of his bed clothes up over his head. He was curled up in the bath still fully dressed under the sheet.

'Jesus, Marshall. What the hell…'

His brother pulled the sheet down, his dark hair a mess. Jimmy thought for a moment that he was looking again at the damaged twelve-year-old boy Marshall used to be, waking up from another night of bad dreams.

'I couldn't sleep in the bed,' Marshall said, putting his hands on the top of the bath and lifting himself up.

'Yeah. And how did you sleep in the tub?'

'I didn't.'

Marshall stepped out onto the tiled floor and ran a hand through his hair. Jimmy stepped forward and embraced him. Marshall dropped his hands to his sides. He never reciprocated an embrace.

'You hungry?' Jimmy asked, stepping back. 'There's a McDonalds across the street,'

'Yeah. Can we?'

'Sure. But listen, we need to be careful. People will be looking for us.'

'What people?' Marshall frowned.

'Police. Maybe some others too.'

Marshall did not respond.

'You understand why?' Jimmy asked.

Marshall nodded.

'Cause we killed those people.'

'That's right. And, you know, if the police catch us they'll separate us. Put us in jail for doing those things.'

'Why will they separate us?'

Jimmy sighed.

'They just will, okay.'

'I don't want that to happen, Jimmy.'

'Me neither. So you understand that we have to make sure no one recognises us. They'll tell the police if they do, you know.'

Marshall nodded though Jimmy was unsure if it had all really penetrated into his brain.

'I'll go get us some burgers,' Jimmy said. 'You need to stay here. Wait for me.'

'Okay.'

They moved into the main part of the room. Marshall lay on his bed and closed his eyes. Jimmy counted his remaining cash. He had less than fifty dollars which wasn't going to last long. He knew that if he used his only credit card or tried to get cash from a bank that the cops would likely be monitoring for activity and would be there in a few minutes. He would need to get cash from somewhere else. He didn't want to think about that right now.

Jimmy lifted Marshall's Patriots cap and pulled the peak down to obscure his face as best he could. He told Marshall he'd be back shortly and to stay put.

When Jimmy was gone, Marshall got off his bed and went to the window. He pulled the curtains open and watched Jimmy walk to the restaurant. He stayed at the window until Jimmy was out of sight then opened the door to the room and ran quickly to the main office. He stopped at the edge of the window looking into the office. There was an older man at the desk this time. He had wanted to see the girl again.

He went back to the room and looked across the lot to the McDonald's. Jimmy came out again carrying a brown paper sack and jogged towards the room. Marshall's face was impassive.

49

Lowe had spent the afternoon at the Blackwater Sheriff's Department on the telephone to his colleagues at the house on Sandy Pond Road and speaking to his superiors at the Boston field office. Early called around all the local law enforcement forces on the Cape checking that they had the FBI alerts and details of the Cain brothers and their car. Some were more up to speed than others. Those that were behind quickly got their act together when Early explained what had happened the previous day.

It was after five before it occurred to Early to ask Lowe where he was going to spend the night. Frank Wood and Randolph Jones had gone home. They had not seen the sheriff all day.

'I hadn't given it much thought,' Lowe told Early.

'You heading back to Boston? I mean, you can direct operations from there, right.'

Lowe looked at his watch.

'Probably best if I stay here. At least for tonight, you know.'

Early figured it would be better for Lowe to go back to his office in Boston and start to collate all that they had and form a proper plan of action. He knew that a plan hatched on the run usually did not get the desired results. Some thinking time was in order and it was likely that the Cain brothers would look to go to ground after what had happened. With no further sightings today, Early thought that they now had some time and space to gather their thoughts. He said as much to Lowe.

'What can I say,' Lowe said, leaning back in the chair usually occupied by Early. 'I like being in the field.'

Early shrugged and told him about the Holiday Inn near his place.

'I can drop you there on the way home.'

'I thought we might grab dinner together. Catch up, you know.'

Early was leaning against the wall just inside the door to the deputies' room.

'Unless you have other plans.'

Early looked out the window and said that he might.

'Yeah,' Lowe said. 'Anything serious?'

'It's definitely serious. Just not how you mean it.'

'You don't want to talk about it.'

Early looked at Lowe and said yes.

The door to the area behind the front desk opened and Shirley Lee shouted along the hall.

'Sheriff's back.'

Early told her that she could go home if she wanted. Shirley Lee said that she did want to and closed the door. Early could hear her shuffling around, getting ready to leave.

'You want to get to the hotel?' Early asked Lowe, stepping away from the wall.

Lowe glanced along the corridor and said that he still had a few calls to make before he was through for the day.

'But you still want a ride?'

'Sure.'

Henry Kapnick pushed the door open at the end of the hall and walked to the doorway where Early stood. He hooked his thumbs under his gun belt and stared at Lowe.

'Special Agent Nick Lowe, FBI,' Lowe said, standing and holding out his hand to greet Kapnick.

The sheriff grasped his hand firmly and shook it. Early looked down and saw the flesh of both men's hands turning white where they gripped each other tightly.

'Early helping you out?' Kapnick asked.

Lowe nodded.

'He says I'm on a task force,' Early said.

Kapnick glanced sideways at him before turning his gaze back to Lowe.

'Big time, huh?' Kapnick said.

'It's a multi-agency task force,' Lowe said. 'These are very serious crimes and I've been told that we need all hands.'

'Well,' Kapnick said. 'You need anything from me just holler.'

He touched the peak of his cap in what looked to Early like an ironic gesture of courtesy and turned to go to his office. He reached the door and paused with his hand on the handle.

'A word, Early,' he said, not turning to look at his deputy.

Early followed Kapnick along the hall and into his room.

'Close the door,' Kapnick said, taking his cap off and running a hand over the top of his head.

Early did as he was told. Kapnick leaned back against the edge of his desk.

'What's he doing here?'

'Who, Nick?'

Kapnick nodded slowly.

'We got some intel that the boys he's after are here.'

'In Blackwater?'

'On the Cape.'

'That's all?'

'Yeah. I mean, what else is there?'

Early's radar was pinging. Lowe seemed to know more about Kapnick than he was willing to say and now Kapnick was getting uptight about Lowe.

Kapnick went around his desk and sat in the chair, switching his computer on and tapping at the keyboard to enter his password.

'You need anything else from me, Sheriff?'

Kapnick said no. Early left the room.

Lowe asked if everything was okay when Early go to the

deputies' room.

'Sure. Why wouldn't it be?'

'No reason.'

'You want that ride now?'

50

Early waited at the hotel until Lowe had secured a room. Lowe was asking the woman at the reception counter for a toothbrush and some toothpaste when Early left. A man could happily wear the same clothes two days in a row so long as he had access to a shower, a toothbrush and maybe some deodorant. Anything else was a luxury.

Early changed into jeans and a blue cotton shirt when he got home. He was hungry and eyed a steak that was chilling in the refrigerator. He decided to call Kate before eating.

'What you been up to now that you're a lady of leisure?' Early asked her when she answered his call.

'Hanging out at my parents' place and hiding my shame from the world.'

'You got no cause to hide from anyone.'

'Always the gentleman, Early.'

'It's the truth.'

'You don't mind seeing me like this, then?'

'No. I don't mind.'

Early wondered if they were both now stepping over the line that he had refused to cross last night when Kate was here. It felt so comfortable with her. He didn't have to force the conversation like he felt he was always doing with other women he had been with. It was easy. Easy was good.

'Have you eaten?' Early asked.

'No.'

'I have steak in the fridge.'

'Just the one?'

'I'll split it with you. Bake a couple of potatoes and pop the caps on some beers. It's nice out. We can eat on the back porch.'

'That sounds nice.'

'You want me to come get you?'

'No. I'll drive.'

Early thought that the place looked a little…ruffled. But he figured it shouldn't look like he made *too* much of an effort, so he let it be. He put four bottles of beer in the freezer compartment to properly chill them and set the steak out on the counter to let it breathe before he cooked it. He turned the oven on, coated two big potatoes in oil, salt and pepper and put them in to bake for an hour. He planned on serving some sliced tomato with the meal but would do that as he was ready to serve.

When he was done with his preparations, Early poured himself a glass of water and went out onto the back porch. He sipped at the water and watched through the trees as a bird at the edge of the pond dipped its beak and rippled the surface of the water. He guessed it must be looking for food. He didn't know what type of bird it was, and didn't much care.

His mind drifted back to the Applegate house. He wondered if they had shared a meal together last night and then gone to bed feeling safe and secure in that big house. Something unimaginable happened after that. How would the woman feel to wake up to the news that awaited her?

Early watched the bird some more and finished his glass of water. He heard car tyres crunch on the track out front and the bird took off into the trees. Looking at his watch, he figured Kate must have left her parent's house straight after their call to be here this soon. He waited till he heard the car door open and close and shouted that he was around back.

Kate came around the corner of the house. She was wearing the same shorts as last night, this time with a loose fitting white cotton top that had ties hanging from the opening at her neck. Her eye was still swollen partially shut and blotches of bruising discoloured her cheek. Early set his empty glass down and waited for her to climb the two steps up onto the porch deck.

'It's beautiful here,' Kate said, looking towards the pond.

'Sure is.'

'You going to offer a girl a beverage?'

'Beer okay?'

'Perfect.'

Kate sat in the chair opposite Early and crossed her legs. She held one hand tentatively to her face and Early was unsure if it was because she was embarrassed to be seen with her injuries or because she was suffering from pain.

'You want a painkiller?' he asked.

'Beer will be fine,' she smiled.

Seventeen-year-old Early Simms first noticed the girl with the long legs and dark hair at Kennedy's on a Saturday lunchtime. It was a hot day at the end of a long summer recess. She was sitting at the counter with a girlfriend, slowly rotating back and forth on her stool. She looked at him when the bell above the door rang as he pushed into the diner ahead of two teammates from the football team. She was wearing denim shorts and a plain white t-shirt. Early had his football practice shorts on and a grey t-shirt adhering tightly to the muscles he had just pushed to their limits in the gym. Her eyes flicked quickly up and down him. He looked at her legs. She was smiling when he looked at her face again. His buddies pushed him towards a booth at the back of the diner.

Early asked who the girl was. He'd seen her at school, he was sure. But she had never looked this good. Early was facing the front of the diner while his friends had their backs to the girl. Both of them turned at the same time – just as Kate looked their way.

'That's Kate Foley,' Andy Prater said.

Prater was a wide receiver on the team, a tall, lean boy who could outrun just about anyone.

The name didn't mean much to Early.

'Her dad's the lawyer,' Prater went on. 'His office is in the square.'

'She looks different,' Early said.

'You mean she looks hotter?' Early's other friend added, grinning.

Sam Baker was a defensive lineman and the biggest guy on the team. He was the first one of them to attempt facial hair that made him somehow cooler.

'Well, yeah. This just happen over the summer or what? I don't remember her looking like that before.'

Baker looked back at Kate again.

'I guess,' he shrugged. 'You want some of that?'

Early looked away as Kate turned to look in his direction.

A car pulled up on the street outside the diner and the driver honked its horn. Kate and her friend got off their stools and went to the door. Kate looked back at Early and then left to get in the car.

Early went onto the porch and was taken back to that day as Kate sat there, twisting hair in one hand. She looked older, no doubt. But age had not dimmed her looks, simply changed them; refined them. She looked a little leaner and had faint wrinkles at her eyes. He didn't really see the damage to her face.

He handed her a beer and took a drink from his bottle. It had been the right decision to chill it in the freezer.

'You got something on your mind?' Kate asked, taking a sip from her bottle.

'No, why?'

'I don't know. I mean, you looked like you weren't quite here just now.'

Early laughed a little.

'What?'

He looked across at the pond.

‘I was thinking about the first time I saw you. I mean, *really* saw you.’

Kate held the cold bottle to her eye and rolled it across the bruised skin.

‘You remember that?’ Early asked, looking at her now.

Kate nodded, holding his gaze.

‘I remember.’

‘At Kennedys?’

Kate took another drink.

‘We only had good times, Early. That’s the thing of it, you know.’

He frowned, not sure of her meaning.

‘After…what happened. You changed. It changed us.’

‘I know.’

‘It was nothing that we did. I didn’t stop loving you. It was just that we were no longer together.’

Early took a drink and swallowed hard.

‘I didn’t want that, Early. But I had to move on with my life. I couldn’t wait around for you to get over it.’

He felt a brief spike of anger and looked at her.

‘*Get over it…*’ he said.

She sat forward and put the beer down on the deck.

‘I never got over it, Kate. I killed someone. He didn’t deserve to die.’

‘No one ever said anything different. But it wasn’t your fault. You might have caused his death, but that doesn’t make you culpable.’

Early pursed his lips and sat heavily on the chair opposite her.

‘That day I came to tell you about college,’ Kate said. ‘You remember that?’

He nodded. Kate sighed and sat back in the chair, pulling her legs up under her. She looked out across his yard. He could see that she was not present for the moment. He waited for her.

‘All I wanted was for you to grab me. To pull me into the house and tell me not to go. Tell me that…’

She curled a hand into a fist and pressed the back of it to her mouth, shaking her head. Early had nothing to say. The sun was starting its long, slow fall into the earth. The early evening light shaded blue to violet.

Early breathed once deeply.

'After the game that day…' he said, looking at Kate.

He saw the memory of that night shine in her eyes.

They said nothing for what seemed like an age.

'You going to cook me dinner or what, deputy?' she said, pulling the hand from her mouth and smiling awkwardly. A tear slipped from one eye and she wiped at it with the heel of her hand.

Early got up and went to the kitchen. When he was out of her line of sight he put both hands on the counter and closed his eyes. He smelled Kate; tasted her in his mouth.

There are times in everyone's life when doors open. Early knew that you always had free will. That you could choose to step through any one of those doors or push it shut again. Once it was shut, it rarely ever opened again.

The door was open now.

He should have walked through it the first time and regretted not having done so. Life could have been very different for both of them if he had.

There was still time to change the future.

51

Officer Brian Scott of the Sandwich PD liked to think of himself as a diligent policeman. He kept his patrol car clean and tidy and his uniform pressed. When he got up in the morning he showered and shaved and dressed quietly in the bathroom so as not to wake his girlfriend, Marney, who was six months pregnant and suffering from back pain that no amount of physiotherapy could shake off. Scott was twenty-seven years old.

He had followed the same routine that morning – with one exception. When he was dressed and ready to leave the apartment, he decided to look in on Marney. She lifted her head from the pillow when he opened the door and waved him into the room. He went to the bed and sat beside her, placing a hand on the small of her back under the warmth of the duvet.

'How you doing?' he asked.

'Okay, I think.'

He moved his hand to her head and pushed strand of hair from her cheek before leaning in to kiss her.

'Have a good day,' he told her.

'Be safe,' she said groggily.

Scott was nearing the end of his shift when he got the call to check out what might be an abandoned car in the parking lot of the CVS Pharmacy on Tupper Road. The store sat at the south end of a large parking lot serving a row of stores off of

Cranberry Highway.

It was dark when Scott stopped his car outside the store. He grabbed a flashlight from the car and walked to the store, which was still open. He spoke briefly to the manager, a heavyset black woman, who told him that the car had been sitting in the lot since before she opened up that morning and had not moved since. It did not belong to any store employees and they had made several PA announcements for any customers who owned the car to identify themselves. No one had.

When Scott asked what made the manager suspicious of a car that had not been in the lot for longer than a single day, she just said that it felt wrong. He had an idea that this was already a waste of his time but thanked the woman and told her that he would check it out.

The car was an old Ford sedan at the northwest corner of the CVS lot. Scott held his flashlight up at shoulder level as he approached the car. He walked around it and saw no obvious signs of anything out of place. There was no accident damage or blood.

He shone the light inside the car. It was not a clean or tidy interior. He thought that he could see what might be bloodstains on the driver's seat and the steering wheel. Maybe the woman had good instincts after all.

Scott went to the front of the vehicle and illuminated the licence plate. The number looked familiar. He thought that he had maybe seen it on a report or something. He keyed the mike on his radio and asked despatch to run a check the number for him. As he waited, he shone the flashlight on the ground around the car. He saw one or two spots of blood.

Thirty seconds stretched to a minute. Stretched to two.

It was taking longer than it should have. Scott keyed his mike again and asked if there was a problem. The dispatcher told him to, uh, wait a minute longer.

He waited, shining his light again at the blood on the ground.

He heard the voice of his Chief of Police on the radio.

That was a first. The chief told him that the car was on an FBI alert relating to two brothers wanted in connection with multiple murders.

Scott listened carefully while he was told to secure the scene and wait for back-up. He acknowledged his orders and looked back at the CVS store. The manager was standing at the door watching him. He nodded at her and she went back inside.

He was going to have to call Marney and tell her that he would be late home.

Real late.

52

The time apart from Kate to fry the steaks and slice the tomatoes had given Early an opportunity to reflect. He was glad of it. He was in no rush to confront the notion that he would be prepared to indulge in anything with a woman who was still married; nor the voice inside his head that said she wasn't really married.

It was a New York strip sirloin and the smell of it sizzling on the griddle pan filled the house. He had the door to the back porch open and smoke from the pan wafted out as darkness fell. The light mounted on the back wall of the cabin was on and flies buzzed in its glow.

'Better that we eat inside now,' Kate said from the doorway.

She had both bottles of beer in one hand. The other hand she put in her hair and pulled it over her head till it mostly hung on one side. Early nodded and went back to the steak, not sure that he could look at her without staring.

When he was sure the steak was done as he liked it, he set it on a plate to rest and turned the gas down. He put the slices of tomato in the cooling pan to cook them a little, soften them up. The fat from the steak spat and hissed as juice from the tomato joined it in the pan.

'Smells good,' Kate said.

'You want to get a couple of plates and set them on the counter?'

Early pointed to the cupboard on the wall to his left.

Kate came around him and stood on tiptoe to reach up for the plates. He smelled her perfume. It was the same one she used to wear all those years ago.

Early served the food when he was ready and they sat together on the far side of the counter that separated the kitchen from the living room, looking out into the back yard. The moon was up and the sky was clear.

Kate asked about Early's work and about his dad. They talked while they ate. When they were finished, Early took the dishes and put them in the dishwasher then closed the back door.

'You want help cleaning up?' Kate asked from her seat across the counter.

Early shook his head.

'I'll get it when you're gone.'

Kate laughed.

'God, that sounded so…I don't know. Final. You want rid of me?'

'No.'

She stood and went to the couch in the living room. Early watched her walk away from him. He didn't want her to leave at all tonight.

Kate did not sit on the couch. She stood with her back to him and looked out of the window at the front of the house.

'There's still time,' she said, not turning to look at him.

Early was unsure if she was talking to him; hoped that she was. He moved to the end of the counter.

'Is there?'

She turned around.

'Best times I ever had were with you, Early Simms. You know that, right?'

'You got married. Those are good times.'

He said it more to remind himself of her status than anything else. He stayed at the end of the counter, eight feet from her.

Kate dropped her shoulders and put her hands into the pockets of her shorts. She crossed one foot over the other and looked at the floor.

'Best I ever had,' she repeated.

She looked at him again. Early put a hand on the counter beside him.

'You want me to stay or go?' Kate asked, her voice dropping low.

Early walked to her, put his hands on her neck and kissed her. Kate's mouth opened on his and it was as if all those years had never happened. He let himself go, not caring about anything except being with her now.

Kate put her hands on his back and pulled Early into her. He felt her body press against him from chest to thigh and burned for her.

Early's mobile phone buzzed on the counter behind them. He pulled away from Kate and went to the phone. She stood where she was, unsure what was happening. He saw it in her face.

'It's always work,' he said, holding the phone up.

Early answered the call. It was Nick Lowe.

'We got the car, Bubba. The Cains' car. It's over in Sandwich. Pick me up at the hotel in ten minutes, okay.'

Lowe hung up without waiting for a response. Early put the phone on the counter.

'I gotta go, Kate.'

'Really?'

'A whole family got killed last night. Two brothers did it. Looks like we've found their car. It's…'

'Go.'

'Kate…'

She wiped at another tear.

He walked forward and embraced her. He felt her shake, her tears soaking the cotton of his shirt. She stepped back and wiped her face with both hands, sniffing loudly.

'I'm a mess,' she said. 'Look at me. A married woman beaten by her husband and now falling into the arms of her first love. It's a bad joke.'

She tried to laugh but it broke into a choked sob.

'This isn't over, Kate. But I'll be gone all night probably. Go back to your parents' place and I'll see you tomorrow. I'll call first chance I get.'

'What about this,' Kate said, holding up her left hand and spreading the fingers to highlight the wedding band still on her hand.

Early shrugged.

'What about it?'

Kate looked at the ring and slipped it off her finger. She put it in the pocket of her shorts, walked to Early and kissed him lightly on the mouth.

'This might end up all sorts of wrong,' she told him.

'I've had enough of wrong in my life.'

53

The house on Oyster Road felt cool when Kate got home from Early's. She went through to the back of the house and saw that the rear door was open. Her mother was at the bottom of the yard in the dark, looking out onto the beach. Kate pressed a switch on the wall beside the door to turn the lights on in the yard. Her mother looked round when the lights came on. Kate waved at her from the open doorway.

Bree Foley was a woman that always appeared somewhat brittle to her friends. When she was not with them, they expressed fears for her mental wellbeing. They speculated that her husband was a serial philanderer – and there had always been rumours around town about the handsome lawyer and his habit of working long hours at the office. Truth was, Bree was not a woman who liked to be demonstrative with her emotions whether good or bad. She largely operated on an even keel and loved her husband very much. She had heard whispers about him but chose neither to believe them nor question Joe about such malicious gossip. She had a good life and enjoyed living it.

Joe had always been closer to their daughter than Bree. She was still unclear why that was. When Kate was growing up, Joe had tried to spend most weekends at home, preferring to put the hours in at work during the week. He was, as a result, always very attentive for those two days. That being said, Bree cared for Kate every day and rejected Joe's suggestion of hiring a nanny to give her time to herself.

She had a child and was committed to looking after her.

'What were you doing out there, Mom?' Kate said to her mother as she came into the kitchen from the yard.

''Enjoying the view. I mean, sometimes it's easy to forget just how privileged we are to have this place and everything that comes along with it.'

Bree went to the sink. She washed her hands in warm water and rubbed moisturiser into them after drying them with a hand towel.

'This must be a pain,' Kate said. 'Having to put up with all of my drama.'

Bree looked at her daughter, pulling tighter the shawl wrapped around her shoulders.

'You might find one day that having kids is all about drama.'

'Come on. Not like this.'

'It's all a matter of degree.'

'You haven't said much about any of this.'

'There's not that much to say is there? I mean, your face speaks for itself.'

Kate pushed her hair off of her face. Bree went to a cupboard and took out a small milk pan. She held it up and asked Kate if she wanted some hot chocolate. Kate said that she did.

'What about the police?' Kate asked as her mother got busy making the chocolate. 'Do you think I should report what John did to me?'

'If it was me, I would. No one should get away with that.'

She kept her back turned to Kate while she spoke, pouring milk into the pan and turning the gas up.

Kate pulled a chair out from the table in the middle of the kitchen and sat down.

'Where did you go tonight?' Bree asked.

Kate thought about lying.

'I went to see Early Simms.'

Bree left the milk to boil and sat in a chair opposite Kate. She looked down at the table and scratched at a small mark on its surface.

'Do you think that's a good idea?' she asked Kate.

'I honestly don't know.'

Bree smiled and looked at her daughter.

'Your dad doesn't like Early. I think his feelings on that subject mostly date from the case he took on when that boy that got killed. He won't admit it. But that's what it really comes down to.'

'And what about you, Mom? What do you think about Early?'

'Does it matter what I think? I mean, really.'

Kate wasn't sure if her mother was now only talking about Early.

'It matters to me. Beyond that, I can't say.'

'I always liked Early. He has character.'

Kate thought that was an old-fashioned way to talk about someone. She had never viewed her mother as being a traditionalist. But it aptly described Early and she nodded slowly.

Bree got up to take the milk off the gas. She sat it on the counter and poured in generous spoonfuls of chocolate powder. Kate watched her stir the liquid till she was happy with it and then take two mugs from a cupboard to fill them with the steaming brew.

They sipped from their mugs, enjoying the quiet of the house.

'Where's dad?' Kate asked, only now realising that she had not seen nor heard her father since she got in.

'He went over to Lane's house.'

'Are you guys okay?'

Bree put her mug on the table.

'When you've been with someone for a really long time,' she said, 'and when your children leave home, you realise eventually that you have a lot of different interests. If you try too hard to push your interests on each other it does not lead to a contented home life. I find it's best to let each other breathe. It can be liberating.'

Kate thought that her father would not have been the one in the relationship to reach that conclusion.

'You didn't ask me what I thought of John,' Bree said.

Kate waited.

'I think you should see Early again,' her mother said.

54

'The woman from the house,' Lowe said to Early as they drove towards Sandwich. 'Missy Applegate?'

Early said he remembered her name.

'She regained consciousness today. I spoke to the hospital.'

'Does she know about her family?'

'Yeah.'

They drove for a mile or so in silence before Lowe spoke again.

'I'm going to see her tomorrow. I'd appreciate it if you came along.'

Early glanced quickly at Lowe and back at the road ahead.

'Sure,' he said. 'What's the plan?'

'I need to see if she can identify the Cain boys.'

'If she saw them.'

Lowe nodded.

'How do you get on with Kapnick?' he asked Early. 'I mean as a boss. What's he like to work for?'

Early shrugged.

'He used to be a bully when he was first in the department. Back when my dad was the sheriff.'

'And now?'

'He's not out on call so much so it's difficult to tell, you know.'

'He's not a hard case with you guys? The deputies I

mean.'

'No, sir.'

'He knows better than to mess with Early Simms, is that it?'

Early concentrated on the road, but he could hear the smile in Lowe's voice.

'The sheriff understands our relationship.'

The car passed under the shadow of the Sagamore Bridge and onto Sandwich Road, heading for Cranberry Highway. Early told Lowe that they would be at the CVS store in maybe five minutes.

'What's your interest in Kapnick?'

'What do you mean?'

'Come on, Nick. What's the story? I work with the man and there are guns in his room. What do I need to know?'

Lowe laughed quietly.

'Tell you what,' he said, 'it comes time that you need to know anything, you'll know.'

'That's comforting.'

There were four police cruisers in the parking lot in front of the pharmacy, all of them in the black and white livery of the local PD. Early pulled to a stop next to the one farthest from the Cains' car where most of police officers were congregated. Staff from the surrounding shops that had closed since the discovery of the car huddled in tight groups around the lot. This much police activity always drew a crowd. The sky was clear, though cool air from the nearby coast kept it from being truly hot.

Early had not bothered to change out of his jeans but had his badge attached to his belt. He had not brought his gun with him. Judging by the rumpled state of Lowe's clothes, Early guessed that the FBI agent had fallen asleep in them on his bed at the hotel. His FBI raid jacket drew attention from the crowd of cops. Early fell a step behind Lowe as they drew near.

Sandwich advertised itself as the oldest town on Cape

Cod. Early had never bothered to look it up, but assumed that it was true. Why say it if not? The population was somewhere around twenty thousand and he knew a couple of the local cops from past contact, but none were more than passing acquaintances. He thought that there were maybe thirty cops or thereabouts in the force as a whole. It was much bigger than the smaller operation in Blackwater. Two men in street clothes broke from the crowd and moved to meet Lowe. They introduced themselves as Detective Sergeant Tramon Sweet and Detective Albert Moss. Early knew they were the only detectives on the local force.

Sweet was not a man whose appearance matched his name. He was a stoutly built black man, fifty years of age and of medium height. He wore his hair short and had a thick goatee beard. His hands were almost as large as Early's despite a difference of several inches in their height. His handshake brought with it a grip of considerable force. Moss was much younger at thirty. He looked more like a school teacher with short brown hair, rectangular framed glasses and a tweed sport coat over black pants.

'Quite a crowd, sergeant,' Lowe said, nodding at the gathering of officers behind Sweet and Moss.

Moss turned slowly to look at the uniformed officers behind him.

'It's a serious business,' Moss said, turning back to Lowe. 'Who's your pal?'

'This is Deputy Simms from Blackwater. He's assisting my task force.'

Moss nodded at Early, acknowledging a fellow local law enforcement officer.

'Nick here is not so bad for a Feeb,' Early said, patting Lowe on the back hard enough to make him take a small step forward.

Sweet laughed while Moss raised a hand to his mouth and turned to the side to hide his reaction. Early thought that an ice-breaker might smooth the way with the locals.

'Who was the first responder?' Lowe asked, trying to

ignore the pain in his back, but grateful to Early nonetheless for what he had done to lighten the atmosphere.

Lowe found that local cops almost always took an immediate and irrational dislike to federal agents as a general rule. Getting past that sometimes took days and that was time they did not have where the Cain brothers were concerned.

'Go get Scott,' Sweet told Moss.

They waited while Moss identified a young cop from the group that was gathered around the car. The man held himself upright and presented well in a neat uniform. Early thought that he had all the external signs of someone who would probably be a good police officer.

Lowe introduced himself and Early.

'Anything you can tell us, officer?' Lowe asked.

Scott looked to Sweet. The detective sergeant told him to go ahead.

'Not much to tell, really.'

Scott recounted the call he received and events at the CVS store before he identified the car with the help of his despatch officer.

'What happened after that?'

'Well, I got told to stay here to secure the scene, which I did. When the guys started to arrive I sent them on a canvas of the stores that were still open. You know, to see if anyone had seen who parked the car.'

'Good thinking,' Lowe said. 'Any luck on the canvas?'

Scott shook his head.

'Nothing. So, after that, we went door to door at the surrounding residences. Wanted to make sure no one was holed up nearby and that they had not stolen another vehicle to replace this one.'

'I'm guessing from the fact that everyone appears to be here now that you didn't find anything?'

'Correct.'

'What about other means of transport. Train or bus or…'

Scott looked at Sweet again. Sweet cleared his throat.

'We'll get on that.'

He gestured to Moss and the detective left them to speak to the gathering of uniformed officers.

'Our main concern,' Sweet said, 'was to make sure those fuckers were not in the vicinity or otherwise causing mayhem in this town. I had all off-duty officers pulled in and sent out on patrol.'

Lowe said that he understood those concerns.

'No adverse reports so far,' Sweet concluded.

'Given their recent history, that's good news,' Lowe said.

55

It was almost three in the morning when Early looked at his watch. He and Lowe were sitting in the office of the chief of Sandwich PD. Early did not feel tired. Lowe looked wired, constantly moving and unable to sit for any length of time.

The office was not ostentatious and smelled faintly of leather and gun oil. It was painted in plain white with a dark wood floor. The furniture was all well-worn: a big wooden desk, a leather swivel chair behind it for the chief, two wooden chairs on the other side of the desk and a couch on the wall between the two windows that overlooked the rear of the property. A large stars and stripes was pinned on the wall just inside the door. The chief faced it every morning when he sat in his chair. Lowe was standing by one of the windows looking through the blinds into the parking lot at the rear of the police building. Two uniformed officers stood by their cruiser talking while one of them smoked a cigarette. The Chief had gone home an hour ago, leaving Detectives Sweet and Moss to continue coordinating the efforts of his officers.

'What do you think, Bubba,' Lowe said. 'Are we close?'

Early did not think that they were and said as much to Lowe.

'Why do you say that?' Lowe asked, turning back to face Early.

'Far as we can tell, that car was abandoned sometime this morning. Correction, yesterday morning. So, they were here, say, twenty hours ago.'

'I guess.'

'And Officer Scott found the car around eight.'

'Correct.'

'They had a minimum of, let's say, twelve hours to get gone from here.'

'Is that what you think they did? That they didn't hang around here.'

'Whatever we might think about these guys, they're not completely stupid. I mean, I think that they abandoned the car in that lot knowing that it would take a while – maybe even more than a day – for anyone to report it as suspicious. That would draw us here.'

'While they go somewhere else?'

'Yes. It's what I would do.'

'Misdirection,' Lowe said, sitting down beside Early.

'There are no reports of any stolen vehicles in the last day, so they must have used some form of public transport. Probably took a bus.'

'I think you're probably right. But I also think that they will not travel far. These boys have likely never been out of the state and in a situation like this will want familiar surroundings.'

'I agree.'

'You think they're still on the Cape?'

Early said that he did not know.

'My money would be on them heading back to the mainland,' Lowe said. 'That's where they will be most comfortable.'

'You might be right.'

'That sounds like you have another theory.'

'I was just thinking, you know. Trying to look at it from their perspective.'

'And?'

Early shifted in his seat and turned to Lowe.

'Everything that happened, all those people they killed, took place on the mainland. They probably figure that anyone looking for them will concentrate their efforts there.'

'Even with the car being here?'

'It's not far from the bridge. And there are more places to hide back there than there are here.'

'That's a lot of thinking for a couple of lowlifes.'

'Like I said, they're not completely stupid.'

They sat quietly for a few minutes. Detective Sweet came into the room and sat heavily on the couch. The sleeves of his shirt were rolled up to the elbows and the top button of his shirt was unfastened.

'Long day,' Lowe said.

'We got nothing,' Sweet said. 'Nothing at the bus station or anywhere else.'

Lowe rubbed his hands over his face. He told them that he needed to call his boss to report in.

Early followed Sweet out of the room and went to the restroom down the hall. He splashed cold water in his face and neck, holding his head over the sink and allowing the water to run into his hair.

He thought about the people that had died at the Applegate house.

And about kissing Kate Foley.

56

The only way to deal with this now, John Lustig knew, was to get face to face with that cunt wife of his. If she thought that she could just cut off his dick and walk away with it in her pocket, well, she did not know John Lustig very well.

It was around midnight when Lustig had come to this realisation. He did not know what time it was now. He found it difficult to keep track.

In his current state of mind, he was not a man that needed to reconsider a decision once it had been made. Nor was it necessary to take much time to prepare. He showered quickly, dressed in a pair of cotton chinos with a shirt and a light sweater. He took a leather wash bag from out of the cabinet in the bathroom and was pleased to see that the gun fit neatly into it. He checked that the magazine was fully loaded, that the safety was properly engaged and zipped it inside the bag. He stood in front of the mirror and looked at himself holding the bag. He smiled.

She wouldn't even see it coming. He saw it playing out: her telling him to leave, him unzipping the bag, pulling out the gun and shooting her point blank in the face. Yeah, that sounded about right.

He picked up his car keys and went out into the hall, forgetting to lock the apartment door. He had too many other things taking up space in his head to be concerned about such mundane details.

57

It was eleven the next morning when the two men arrived at the hospital to see Missy Applegate. She was pushing cold scrambled eggs around a plate on the tray fixed over her bed. The doctors had come to the conclusion that she had suffered a concussion rather than anything more serious. She lightly touched the dressing on her head where the bullet had sheared its way through her scalp. She felt the rough pattern of sutures holding her head together. There were nineteen in total, she knew.

Yesterday was mostly shrouded in fog. She had slept fitfully throughout the course of the day with the help of sedatives. Her dreams became less coherent though the same themes remained: of fear, loss and death.

Missy remembered seeing a TV program one time where the surviving victims of violent crime were interviewed. She thought at the time how awful it must have been for those people to lose their friends and family so suddenly with no time to say goodbye. Or I love you. Those people all told a similar story: about how they would wake up in the morning and for a few brief moments, before sleep left them entirely, would not recall the horror of what had happened. Then it would hit like a sledgehammer, taking the air from their lungs.

Missy would have gladly traded one of her limbs to experience such momentary ignorance. She wasn't looking for joy, merely the absence of pain.

Every waking moment and sleep filled interval for Missy was a hateful reminder of her loss.

Sure, she knew that Hank had not been the perfect husband. However, she truly believed that he had been faithful to her and to their life together. He was a man of the highest calibre, she was certain. It made his passing all the more senseless, for a man like that to be killed by men who were not fit to share the Earth.

And her beautiful boy.

The boy in the cow jammies.

Pushing at her back; 'mooove over, Mommy.'

Laughing a child's laugh.

Life before Hank had been good to Missy. Her family was wealthy. She had never known her parents having to work like everyone else. Their fortune came from the efforts of her grandparents and all that anyone in the family had to do now was manage the riches that they partly administered through a charitable foundation. Missy was going to take over from her father next year. Her younger brother was too busy travelling the world and screwing his way through his trust fund. Missy often wondered if he was a happy man. Was that what men wanted? Did Hank yearn for such a life? He did not appear to.

Now he was dead.

Missy was an emotional woman in every sense. What coursed through her veins now burned like acid, prickling her skin and roiling in her blood. The pure, dreadful force of her anger was something that Missy had not experienced before. Her final dream this morning, before the cop outside the door woke her with his inane banter with one of the female nurses, was unlike the others that had gone before it. The dream was raw and red; of pain and torn flesh rendered under Missy's own hands.

The two men that came into Missy's room could not have been more different. The smaller of the two wore crumpled pants and a shirt that looked like it had not been washed in a few days. His FBI jacket was buttoned almost to the top, as if he was trying to hide what he wore underneath.

The big man looked tired. But he presented like someone who would always have a shower and a shave no matter how he felt. His deputy's uniform looked fresh and she smelled the polish from his leather belt and holster. He was clearly outranked by the shorter man but did not carry himself other than as a man who was always in control. He reminded her a lot of Hank in that way.

The FBI agent introduced himself as Special Agent Lowe and told her that the other man was Deputy Simms. The agent spoke as she imagined he would. There was the expected stuff about how they were doing everything they could to track down the men that had done this to her. It was 'tireless' this and 'relentless' that. Missy nodded at the appropriate times. All the while, that acid inside her fizzed and burbled. She knew that she would not be able to contain it much longer before she screamed.

She noticed Deputy Simms staring at her. She wondered if he could see into her, through the layers of flesh and fat and muscle and into the core of her being. She felt vaguely uncomfortable under his watchful gaze, certain that he could read the dark of her thoughts.

'Do you recognise any of these men?' Lowe asked, pushing her breakfast plate to the side and laying out a number of photographs in front of her. They were all taken at some law enforcement office – except one. He looked different, his eyes unfocused and not quite looking into the camera lens. She noticed a certain resemblance between that man and another. There was a Boston Police mark on the photograph of the other man and what appeared to be a serial number. She wondered if they were related.

'Sorry,' she said, shaking her head. 'I don't know these men.'

'Are you sure?' the deputy asked. 'Why don't you take your time and look again.'

Missy glanced sideways at him and felt that

uncomfortable scrutiny again. He seemed earnest in his desire to get something from her.

She self-consciously put her hand on the photograph of the man she had first noticed, the vacant looking man.

'Do you recognise him?' the deputy asked.

She heard his voice change a little. His body inclined forward.

'No,' Missy said, handing the photos back to Lowe. 'I don't recognise anyone.'

Lowe nodded and put the photographs in his jacket pocket, looking like he was getting ready to leave. The deputy stepped forward until he was right beside the bed.

'The men that came to your house,' he said to Missy, 'may have killed some other people. The girl's parents.'

Missy looked down at her hands.

'I know you're hurting right now,' Simms went on, 'but the fact is I can see more than hurt in your eyes.'

Missy looked at him now.

'I see anger too. And I understand that feeling, I really do. But it is not something that you should act upon.'

'I don't—' Missy started.

'We know the line of business your husband was in,' Simms said, cutting her off by raising a hand, 'and that he will have had men that were loyal to him. And probably to you. Grief can make a person do things that they would not otherwise do.'

Missy held his gaze, aware that in doing so she was only making her fury more apparent to him. Then he did something unexpected. He reached out and took hold of one of her hands and crouched beside the bed until his eyes were level with hers.

'Let us do the hunting, Mrs Applegate. If you do that, I promise we will get these men. I will see justice is done for your family.'

'You mean catch them?'

'Whatever happens is up to them.'

Missy felt him squeezing her hand gently.

'You'll let us do that for you?' the deputy asked.

Missy felt herself becoming undone by this man's kindness; felt her anger dissipating. She knew that the anger would be replaced by a sadness she may not be able to bear. But as much as she wanted to grasp her fury and hold it to her to keep the grief at bay, she felt it slipping from her as if his very touch was drawing it away.

'Did you see the men that did this to you?' the deputy asked.

She shook her head, tears slipping out of her eyes and spilling down her cheeks.

'Okay,' he said, standing and letting go of her hand.

Missy wiped at her face and looked up at him.

'There won't be any catching these men,' she said, her voice ragged. 'I mean you know that, right, deputy?'

Simms rubbed the underside of his chin with the back of his hand.

'You've been to my house haven't you?' her voice breaking now with sobs. 'You've seen what they are capable of.'

'I've been there,' he told her. 'I saw it.'

This time she grabbed his hand, squeezing hard with both of hers. She felt strength in his grip.

'There's no catching,' she said. 'You just get them. Do you understand me? Get them for Hank and for Jordan.'

She let go of his hand and, drained of all of her strength, covered her face and sobbed uncontrollably.

58

Early got home around four in the afternoon, feeling drained from the visit to Missy Applegate. There had been no further leads on the Cain brothers from the Sandwich PD or anywhere else Early's view was that they would surface again soon and maybe it was no bad thing that it happened a little while later – putting some distance between their crimes and their arrest. It would make everyone on both sides less likely to act in anger or haste.

Lowe was heading back home to Boston to catch up with his team and get some fresh clothes. He told Early that he would be back tomorrow morning. Early did not think that Lowe being in Blackwater was going to assist them much, but he said nothing about that to Lowe. He did wonder if Lowe's desire to be here had more to do with whatever he had going on with Kapnick than with the Cain investigation.

Early called Kate when he got home. He wanted to hear her voice before he did anything else, feeling like a teenager again. When she answered his call, he told her about the last twenty-four hours; all of it spilled out in a rush.

'Slow down, Early. We've got plenty of time.'

'It doesn't feel like that to me sometimes.'

'I'd like to see your dad,' she told him.

That took him by surprise.

'When?'

'Now.'

Early looked at his watch.

'Would that be okay?' Kate asked.

'I don't know. I guess. Why do you want to see him?'

'He was always nice to me. And, I don't know, it just feels like I should.'

'You realise that he probably won't know who you are. I mean, he rarely recognises me now.'

'I understand.'

'Give me some time to get changed and I'll come get you.'

Kate came out the front door of her parents' house before Early had time to get out of his car. She skipped down the steps and walked quickly round to the passenger side of the car.

'You don't want your dad to see me?' he asked.

She waved a hand at him as she fastened her seatbelt.

'It's not that.'

She clicked her belt in place and put her hand on top of his. Early nodded; a tacit acknowledgement that they would both leave that particular conversation for another time. He was happy to see her and did not want to sour it.

'Is it far from here?' she asked. 'To your dad's place.'

Early liked that she called it his 'place'.

'Twenty minutes maybe. I called ahead and told them to make him presentable.'

When they were on the highway, Kate slid the window down on her side letting the warm, passing air tousle her hair. Early always liked that about her - that she was not too precious about her appearance the way some women were. She didn't mind getting her hair or make-up messed up.

'It must have been tough for you,' Kate said. 'You know, with your mom gone and then your dad getting sick. I forget sometimes how lucky I am to have both of my parents still around.'

'I think it would have been harder if my dad had died. We looked after each other after mom was gone. He helped me out getting the house fixed up. It was a man thing, you know.'

'The work took your mind off the pain?'

'Something like that, yeah. More so for him, you know. I mean, they'd been married a while.'

'Did you ever think we would? Get married, I mean.'

Early's mouth opened but no sound came out. Kate laughed. It was full blooded and open mouthed, as if his reaction had taken her by surprise. Early felt a flush or embarrassment on his neck.

'Not really,' he said. 'I mean we were just kids.'

'I thought about it.'

He looked over at her. She was staring out of the open window.

'You're a girl,' he told her. 'Girls think about that kind of stuff more.'

She turned to him.

'You know all about girls, now, Early Simms.'

'I know about you,' he shrugged.

'I suppose that you do.'

59

A male attendant at the nursing home walked along a wide hallway ahead of Early and Kate. The floor was tiled and the place felt cool. The hall was painted in a pale shade of blue with white doors at regular intervals. The rooms had the occupant's name on a card inside a plastic holder screwed to the wall outside. There were no permanent nameplates here.

The attendant stopped at the last door on the right and knocked lightly before pushing at the door. He waited inside, holding the door open for Early and Kate.

'You got visitors Mr Simms,' the man said.

Charlie Simms was sitting at a small, round table beside a large window looking out into the garden of the home. It was getting to dusk. There was a couch beside the table and at the other end of the couch was a small kitchenette with a counter to separate it from the rest of the room. A bed with a handrail was on the wall inside the door. A TV mounted on the wall opposite the bed was tuned to a local sports channel. The sound was muted.

Charlie Simms turned when he heard the attendant's voice. His eyes went to Early first. There was no spark of recognition. For perhaps the first time Early was not immediately disheartened by that. A broad smile spread across Charlie's face when he saw Kate. He stood from his chair and walked forward, embracing her. Kate looked at Early and put her arms around Charlie, unsure how to react.

'Take it easy there, Mr Simms,' the attendant said, closing

the door and nodding at Early as he left.

Charlie stepped back from Kate.

'Is Early here with you?'

The smile remained on his face. Early saw it in his eyes also and was pleased to see his father looking like his former self. It did not matter to him that he had not been the one to be embraced.

'He might be along later,' Kate said.

'Playing football, no doubt. That boy cares more about the game than anything else. But don't you let him ignore you.'

'I won't, sir. Don't you worry.'

Charlie nodded, satisfied with the answer. His eyes flicked uncertainly to Early and his smile faltered. Early could see confusion descending on his father and it broke his heart.

'This is my cousin,' Kate said, quickly. 'He gave me a ride here.'

Charlie grasped Early's hand and shook it firmly, the smile returning.

'Good to meet you, son,' he said.

'You too,' Early answered.

Charlie ushered Kate to the couch. She put a hand on Early's arm and then followed Charlie, sitting beside him on the couch.

Early went to the television and clicked it off. He stood facing the wall for moment to compose himself. On the couch, Charlie asked Kate how her father, Joe, was. Early had not been certain to that point if his father had truly recognised Kate.

Early sat on the bed and allowed his dad the freedom to speak to Kate. They talked for a while about how Kate was getting on at school and did she have any plans for college. Early listened without interrupting until he saw the signs that His father's mind was starting to slip again. Charlie started to get agitated, frowning and looking to Early and back at Kate, fear etched plainly on his face.

Early stood and made a point of looking at his watch before telling Kate they had to get back. Kate got up and Charlie went with them to the door. Kate kissed his cheek and said she would see him later. Charlie looked at his son.

'Do you go to school with my boy?' he asked, his eyes searching Early's face.

'Yes, sir.'

'You tell him to hold onto this one,' he said, pointing at Kate. 'He's not careful, she'll up and leave him.'

'I'll make sure that he gets the message.'

They walked in silence back to the car. Early felt a bubble of pressure build in his chest before it moved to his throat. He got in the car feeling as if the bubble would choke him of oxygen. Kate got in beside him and closed the door.

'I didn't know it would be like that,' she said. 'I'm so sorry, Early.'

He grabbed her and pulled her into an embrace, trying to breathe through his pain. Kate put her arms around him, one hand going up to his head and through his hair. She could feel his body heaving against her and held him tight until he was still again.

60

He was quiet on the drive back to town. Kate did not know what to say about what had happened at the home. She was unsure if Charlie's recognition of her had been a good thing. Initially, after Early pulled away from her embrace, she had thought that he was happy Charlie had at least recognised something from his old life, even though it had not been his son. Now, she wondered if Early was falling into one of the brooding silences that marked out his behaviour as a young man. He had been prone to pulling back within himself and internalising his feelings.

Kate was no longer sure at all that what had nearly happened between them the previous night was what Early wanted. She wanted him more than she could ever remember wanting to be with a man; more so than that night after Jerod Butler died. But this now felt more like the last day between them, Early sullen and uncommunicative.

'You can drop me back at your parents if you want time to yourself,' Kate said as they passed a sign welcoming them to Blackwater.

'No, that's okay.'

Early found it difficult to keep his voice even when he spoke so he stuck to short answers. His body had been hot and shaking after the visit with his father, only easing after the embrace with Kate. As he drove into town, he felt his hands tingle on the steering wheel and was aware of his body temperature rising again. He could feel sweat on his back where it met the car seat. Kate was quiet, crossing and uncrossing her legs. He heard the sound of her skin moving and gripped the wheel tight.

'You've been quiet,' she said as he turned off the highway towards his cabin.

'I know.'

'Are you sure that you don't want to take me home? I mean it's okay if you do. I understand.'

He shook his head. Kate was not certain what to make of that gesture and told him so. She hated that the phone call last night interrupted what was happening and that he had had to leave. She had felt on the brink of something good. Now it felt lost.

'What's the problem?' she asked him, sounding more confrontational than she had intended.

Early huffed out a breath and she sensed the anger in that gesture. He pulled the car to a hard stop outside the cabin, the wheels slipping on the dirt sending stones into the undergrowth.

She followed him to the house, almost skipping to keep up with his stride. She used to hate it when he got like this back then. She had to pull so hard to drag his feelings out. It was what she got tired of eventually.

'I'm going for a shower,' he said when they were inside, not even looking back at her as he pulled open the door to the bathroom.

Kate followed him, putting a hand out to stop the door from closing. Early turned sharply; Kate grabbed his shirt pulling him into her.

He pulled at her clothes as their mouths opened together. She slipped her hand down his belly and over his jeans until she felt his hardness. The rest of it was too fast but neither of them wanted to slow it down. It was about lost time and longing.

Early lifted her with their mouths still together and took her into the bedroom. He pushed her shorts and underwear down. Kate stepped out of her clothes when they fell to the floor. She watched as he undressed, his body not much changed from when she used to know it intimately. He was not as lean any more, but still powerfully built.

He sensed that she wanted to control it, but her desire was no match for his.

When he had her on the bed, Early kissed her long and hard, feeling her hand moving on him. He slid down her body, lingering slowly as he went before cradling her in his mouth. Kate moved against him, her body lifting off the bed and arching at the end as she convulsed.

Early moved up on the bed and pushed inside of her.

He stared at her face and felt her hands on his back. Her legs were tight against him, urging him on.

Something white-hot flashed behind Early's eyes. He closed them tight and strained his whole body.

Neither of them spoke after as they lay side by side on the bed. Kate curled into him and he pulled her close with an arm around her shoulder. He sensed nothing but her taste and smell and wondered how it was that he had ever allowed her to leave all those years ago.

61

Marshall Cain watched his brother sleeping in the flickering light from the TV screen. The room smelled of used burger wrappers and sweat. Marshall knew that Jimmy would want him to stay in the room, but he couldn't stop thinking about that girl – the one at the motel reception. It wasn't fair that Jimmy got to talk to her and he did not.

He went to the door and opened it as quietly as he could. Jimmy did not stir, his chin resting on his chest and his face muscles slack. Marshall was sure that he was out pretty good.

It was pleasant outside, the air still holding some of the day's heat and the path cool under his bare feet. Marshall left the room door ajar and walked towards the light from the office. He stopped at the edge of the window hoping that she would be there this time. She was – leaning on the counter reading a magazine. Her top was loose and hung down. He could see the swell of her breasts in the white bra she wore.

Marshall had felt unfulfilled since that night in the car with the Chalk girl. This girl made him feel the way that Brianna had before she ran; before Jimmy shot her.

He watched from the window. His eyes were wide, almost completely black as his pupils expanded.

Jimmy wouldn't want him here, looking at this girl.

But Jimmy wasn't right all the time. He thought he was, but he didn't know all that Marshall wanted or needed. Not even close.

62

'I got a job for you, Manu,' Henry Kapnick told Polite over the phone.

The call had woken Polite and his mouth felt thick, the taste of blood lingering with each swallow. Manu Polite knew that Kapnick had broken his jaw. He'd had broken bones before and knew what it felt like.

'You there?' Kapnick asked.

'I hear you,' he said, through gritted teeth. 'What's this about?'

'Not on the phone. I'm coming over.'

Kapnick ended the call abruptly. Polite got up slowly from his bed and went to the bathroom. He stood in front of the mirror and opened his mouth, running a finger over his teeth and around the inside of his cheek. It came back with blood on it. He sniffed hard and spat bloody saliva into the sink, turning the cold water on to wash it away. He leaned down and took a mouthful of water from the faucet, rinsing it around his mouth and slowly releasing it into the running water.

Polite had killed one man in his lifetime. He was seventeen and running with a gang when there had been a mass brawl. Most of his crew had brought a weapon and he was no different, taking a six-inch knife from his mother's kitchen. He got into it with one of the biggest kids in the other crew and was on the wrong end of a good beating when he pulled the knife and stabbed the kid five times fast in the chest. He punctured the heart and the boy staggered away from him out into the street where he collapsed and died. Polite had dropped the knife into a storm drain and no one on either side had spoken to the cops. It went the way of so many young men's deaths in such situations: a tragic footnote in a local newspaper.

That killing was not something that he had thought about in advance. He'd been in many fights and won a lot more than he had lost so knew the game. But the oldest kid in his gang had told everyone to come ready that night and he had a sense that the kid he came up against was not going to stop until he was out cold – and maybe not even then. In his head, Polite justified it as self-defence.

Sheriff Henry Kapnick aroused similar feelings in Polite now. He had a sense Kapnick was going to keep coming after him unless he did something about it. But killing a cop was not an easy thing to get away with and right now Polite could not conceive of a plan that would achieve the twin aims of killing Kapnick and keeping his ass out of jail for the rest of his life.

Polite opened the door a half hour later and stepped back to let Kapnick into the apartment. Kapnick looked at the swelling on Polite's face and made a tutting sound.

'You should get that looked at, Manu. Could be you broke something.'

'I'll survive.'

Kapnick went to the kitchenette area, opened a cupboard and took out a plastic cup. He held it up to the light before filling it with cold water from the faucet and drinking it down in one long pull. Polite sat on the end of his bed and waited.

Kapnick burped and dropped the cup into the sink.

'Hot out there,' he said.

'You said you had to talk to me.'

Kapnick leaned on the counter that separated the kitchenette from the rest of the apartment. He took his hat off and wiped sweat from his forehead with a handkerchief. Polite had seen Kapnick in this mode before: building up to his revelation. It was a control thing, he knew and it bored Polite.

'We've got a problem,' Kapnick said.

'What kind of problem?'

'One that needs a permanent resolution.'

Polite rubbed his hands together before cracking his knuckles.

'You need me to spell it out?' Kapnick said, walking around the counter towards Polite.

'No.'

'Don't you want to know the details?'

'I figure you'll get to telling me.'

Kapnick put his hat back on and hooked his thumbs into his belt. Polite thought that maybe the sheriff had put on some weight in the last year. The belt looked a little bit tighter on his gut.

'It needs to look…random. Messy.'

'I understand.'

Kapnick tilted his head over to one side.

'You do know that I'm telling you to kill a man?'

'I know.'

'Cause you seem awful calm about it.'

'It is what it is.'

'You done it before?'

Polite looked up at Kapnick as he spoke.

'I done it. It's not a thing.'

Kapnick stared at Polite as if trying to work out if he was telling the truth.

'Who is it? Polite asked.

'Guy called Nick Lowe.'

Manu frowned.

'Do we know him?'

'*I* know him and that's enough.'

'What he do?'

'It's what he wants to do to me that I'm worried about

right now. I need it done soon.'

Kapnick reached behind his back and pulled out an old, scratched revolver. He held it out to Polite.

'I pulled this from evidence and erased the record of it. It was an old case from years ago. No one will be able to trace it.'

Polite took the weapon from Kapnick and turned it over in his hands. He pushed the cylinder open and saw that it was fully loaded.

Kapnick went to the door and pulled it open. Sunlight shafted in, dust motes dancing in the air.

'I'll tell you where he'll be. And make sure you empty that thing into him. Do it right.'

63

The phone rang in the living room, pulling Early from sleep. He looked at Kate next to him and rested a hand on her shoulder. She did not stir. He slid out from under the covers, pulled on a pair of gym shorts and left the room, closing the door quietly. He did not immediately recognise the number displayed on the phone screen, except that he knew it was local.

'It's Bree Foley, Early. How are you today?'

Early walked through the kitchen to the rear door of the cabin and went out onto the porch.

'I'm good.'

'Is my daughter there with you?'

Early could not read the tone of her voice.

'She is, yes.'

Early sat on the steps leading down to the yard and enjoyed the rising warmth of the day on his skin.

'I didn't see you around much when Kate went to school in Boston,' Bree told him. 'There was that business with the court action and with Joe…'

'I understand that it was difficult for everyone.'

'I've seen you in your patrol car, of course. And sometimes walking in town when you're off duty.'

'I like it here.'

'I guess you must. How's your dad doing?'

Dying.

'He's ok, you know. Considering…'

'He was a good man.'

'Does Mr Foley know that you're calling here?'

'Joe? No, he's gone to play golf.'

'It must be nice. Being retired, I mean. Having all that time to yourself.'

A bird landed in Early's yard about twenty feet from the porch. It stared at him and then pecked at the ground. A breeze blew across the yard and Early smelled the ocean on it.

'You seem different now, Early. Something… I don't know.'

Early felt himself shrug.

'Did you miss playing football?'

'Not at the time, no. I never wanted to put the pads on again. Now? I wish I had done something about it. I mean, gotten some help. Talked to someone about it, I guess.'

'What did you like so much about it?'

The juddering impact of a tackle. Inflicting violence on another person.

'Difficult to say now. It's been so long I barely remember.'

'Know what I think?'

'No.'

'I think you're a man out of time Early Simms. By hundreds of years. I mean I saw you play football and people were genuinely afraid of you. For good reason. You were a gladiator.'

Early turned at the sound of the porch door opening. Kate stood in the doorway, her body swamped by one of his t-shirts. He could still see the curves underneath where the fabric met her skin. She smiled at him. He was transported.

'Is she there with you right now? Kate, I mean?'

Early stared at Kate.

'Yes,' he said into the phone.

'Will you take care of her?'

'Yes.'

'I believe that you will. Thank you, Early.'

Early pressed the end call button and stood, stretching his arms above his head. Kate walked to him and put her arms tight around him.

'That was your mom.'

'She checking up on me?'

'I honestly don't know. Felt more like she was checking up on me.'

'She's a good soul.'

Early put an arm around Kate and turned her to go back into the house.

'You could be right,' he said.

64

They ate eggs and toast on the porch, drinking orange juice in the bright morning sun and enjoying being together. Early knew that had they stayed together back then it would not have turned out like this. A lot would have happened in those years – good times and bad times. Maybe kids. Maybe divorce. Now felt like the right time for them.

'This is nice,' Kate said getting up and walking onto the yard, feeling the grass under her feet.

She lifted her face to the sky and enjoyed the warmth on her skin. She heard birds down by the pond and only the faintest hum of traffic from the nearby road. She turned back to the house and was struck by the thought that if she could go back on her life she would not change a single thing about it if this was where she was destined to be. Early looked so good lounging on a chair in only his shorts, squinting at her through the sunlight. He had done such a good job with the place. Him and his dad.

Kate went to Early and leaned down to kiss him. She drew back and looked at him for a moment.

'What?' he asked.

'You did okay, Early. I mean, with the house and where you've ended up. Are you happy?'

'I think I am now.'

She smiled.

'I'm going for a shower.'

Early put the breakfast dishes in the dishwasher and wiped the work surfaces. It was already after ten but today he didn't care about getting to the office on time. Kapnick was preoccupied with whatever it was that he was into and if anything broke on the Cain brothers he figured that Nick Lowe would be on the phone straight away.

Not for the first time, the proximity of Lowe and Kapnick in all of this weighed on Early's mind. Notwithstanding his work as a law enforcement officer and all that he saw of human nature, he generally thought the best of most people. That was, until they disappointed him. He wondered if Lowe had called him to join their task force not for any of the skills that he could bring to the investigation but more to give Lowe a reason to come to Blackwater and keep tabs on Kapnick.

Early went to the living room, picked up his laptop and sat on the couch. He opened his web browser and entered a search for the Boston FBI field office where Lowe was based. He found the main switchboard number and entered it on his phone. A man answered and Early asked to speak to Special Agent Lowe.

'Hold, please.'

Some bland music played while he waited.

'Anti-corruption task force,' a male voice said when he was connected. 'This is Special Agent Hostetler.'

'I was looking to speak to Agent Lowe.'

'He's, uh, not here right now, sir. Who's calling?'

'Do you know where I can find him?'

'I can't give you that information, sir. Can you let me know who this is and I can get a message to him?'

'Is he on assignment or something?'

'I really can't say. But if you let me have your name…'

'Tell him Deputy Simms called from Blackwater.'

There was a moment of silence on the other end of the phone.

'Say, what is it that you guys do on the corruption task force?' Early asked.

'Anti-corruption.'

'Sure, that's what I meant.'

'It kind of says it all in the title, Deputy Simms.'

'I mean, do you look at corruption in public service. You know, in law enforcement agencies.'

'Uh, sure. Yes, that's part of it. Listen, do you still want me to tell Agent Lowe that you called?'

'Yeah, thanks.'

Early ended the call and waited. He didn't think it would take long for Lowe to get the message and call him. He listened to the sound of Kate in the shower. He knew that real life would impinge upon them soon, that they would have to deal with her husband. But for now he wanted to enjoy what they had.

Lowe called almost exactly five minutes after the end of Early's call to the Boston field office.

'I understand that you were looking for me,' Lowe said, the tension apparent in his voice.

'Right. I asked them to get a message to you.'

'What was that message, Early?'

'Sounds to me like you know. I don't appreciate being used, Nick.'

'That's not what's happening.'

'It sure feels like it. But why don't you explain it to me.'

'I'd prefer to do it face to face.'

'Okay. But tell me one thing, are you even a part of the task force on the murders out at that house or was that just a convenient cover?'

'That's not fair, Early.'

'Three people died at that house. I don't think it's fair on them, do you?'

'This is why we should talk in person. I'll come down today.'

'Meet me at the diner across from the office.'

'What time?'

'Make it at one. You can buy me lunch.'

Kate came out of the bathroom in Early's t-shirt with her

hair wrapped in a towel. Early put his phone down and closed the laptop. Kate saw the look on his face.

'Bad news?' she asked.

'We'll see.'

65

Early left Kate at the cabin and drove to town in his department cruiser. She was happy to have time alone away from her parents, able to take life at her own pace for a change. She said she would call in to her office. She was keen to see how things were back at work. Early took it as good sign; that she was starting to think again about getting on with normal life. She did not appear to have any of the tell-tale signs of post-traumatic stress disorder that can take over a person's life after a violent incident like the one she had endured. He had seen it many times with victims of crime. He knew it himself, recognising that it was probably what happened to him after Jerod Butler's death.

He used the car radio to call ahead to the office to see what the day had in store.

'Got a report of a break-in at Crabbies on twenty-eight North,' Shirley Lee told him. 'Sheriff told me to send Frank out.'

Crabbies was a seafood restaurant that Early had been to once or twice. He knew where it was.

'I'll take it,' Early told her. 'I'm already on the road.'

'Okay. I'll let them know.'

'I'll call in when I get there.'

He was glad to have the opportunity to stay out of Kapnick's way until after he met Lowe. If there was an ongoing investigation into the sheriff by the FBI's anti-corruption task force it probably meant that Kapnick was into something pretty heavy. Early wondered if any of his fellow deputies were caught up in it.

He turned right onto Elm road, taking him away from the town centre and towards Highway 28. He lifted his sunglasses from the centre console and put them on. It was going to be another hot day.

After dressing, Kate poured herself a glass of water and went onto the back porch. It was becoming her favourite place to be. She turned one of the chairs so that it faced out into the yard and sat with her feet up on the railing, sipping at the water.

She had called her mother when Early left and told her that she was going to spend the day at the cabin. Her mother said that she thought that was a good idea. They skirted around last night and the fact that Kate had spent it with Early.

'Have you heard from John?' her mother had asked.

'No.'

'That's good. Best thing would be for him to just move on.'

'I know. But I can't read him any more. I guess I never really could.'

'You live as long as me, you get to thinking you never really know anyone. I mean, what they might be capable of.'

'Not even your kids?'

Bree Foley laughed.

'I'm only now beginning to see what you're capable of, honey.'

'And?'

'Ask me again in a couple of years.'

66

He woke with a start at the sound of a car door being closed. John Lustig looked up and saw Joe Foley walking to the back of his car, opening the trunk and lifting a golf bag onto his shoulder. Lustig sat up in his car and rubbed at his eyes. He checked his watch and figured he must have been asleep for close to three hours. He felt better for it, clear of purpose.

Joe Foley leaned forward to account for the weight of the bag and walked up to the front door of the house on Oyster Road. Lustig was parked sixty metres or so along the road. He had recognised his wife's car in the driveway when he pulled past the house in the dark early hours of the morning. He was happy to wait her out.

Lustig reached under the driver's seat and lifted his handgun from the leather wash bag. He checked again that it was fully loaded, releasing the catch that allowed the magazine in the handle to slide out into his palm. He shoved the magazine back in place and switched the safety off.

No point in being unprepared.

He put the weapon down on the passenger seat, opened his door and got out to stretch. He'd been sitting in that seat for a long time and needed to move around to loosen up. A woman walked past with a dog on a leash. Lustig smiled at her and said that it was a lovely morning. She smiled hesitantly, nodded and walked on past him. He thought that maybe she had quickened her pace.

Back in the car, Lustig turned his key in the ignition and

set the air conditioning to its highest setting. He closed his eyes and enjoyed the cool air on his face.

He was in no rush.

67

It had been a frustrating morning for Early at Crabbies. There was no doubt that someone had broken into the restaurant during the night and busted open the tills to steal a couple hundred dollars, but the video cameras in the premises were not operational and the chances of finding any other useable evidence was slim. He went through the necessary motions, taking statements and making reassuring noises to the owners, Bud and Catherine Freeney. But it was a dance they all knew.

Early checked in with the office by radio. It seemed like a quiet day so far, which was fine by him. He called Kate after he had spoken to Shirley Lee.

'You want to get a coffee and some pie later?' he asked her. 'I have to meet Nick Lowe, the FBI agent, in Kennedy's at one but I don't think that will take long. We can meet after that. Maybe I'll take the afternoon off.'

'That all sounds just fine to me. What time is it now?'

Early checked his watch.

'Just gone twelve.'

'Can you pick me up? I need to buy some clothes so I'll do some shopping in town while you meet with the agent.'

'Yeah, okay.'

She was quiet for a moment.

'Listen,' she said, 'I'm going to have to deal with John eventually. My husband.'

'I know that. But not today, huh?'

'Sure. It'll wait.'

Nick Lowe considered himself a man of principle and a true professional. He took real pride in his work. His father had been a Boston city cop and his older brother had followed their father onto the force. He knew about service and duty and didn't need Early Simms to lecture him on it. But he had undoubtedly not been straight with his friend and he wanted to clear the air.

Lowe had enrolled at the FBI Academy straight out of college. He wanted something different from his father and brother and took to the work of an agent like a natural. He was recognised as a real up and comer and had ambitions beyond fieldwork. He thought that he might parlay his law enforcement experience into politics at some point – but only after his kids were older.

Lowe met his wife, Carly, while at the Academy. She was there working on a research project for a college professor who was writing a book on the history of the Agency. It was her first bit of real work after college and as an English literature graduate it suited her fine, though it did not pay well. Lowe had seen her around the Academy campus and their relationship developed quickly after their less than auspicious first date – a burger dinner and a few too many beers at a nearby bar.

Ten years and two kids later, Lowe was happy with life. Carly had suffered depression after the birth of their oldest daughter four years ago but she had recovered and was doing a little freelance research work from home. He had encouraged her to get back to it because he knew that she was unfulfilled now that the girls were growing.

'You have to make it right. Nick,' Carly had told him this morning after the call with Early.

She was always his sounding board. He felt grounded by her.

'I know. And I plan to. That's why I wanted to meet him today.'

'Tell him you're sorry and don't qualify it. You know how you do that.'

He knew.

'I'll try.'

Lowe got to Blackwater and pulled into a free parking space at the sheriff's office. Kapnick's car was there and he did not want to have to speak to the man at the moment. He went straight to Kennedy's and ordered a Coke though he was twenty minutes too soon for the meeting with Early.

Pat Kennedy called him 'Special Agent' with a grin and served him his Coke. Lowe took it to a table at the front of the diner so that he could watch the street. He called Roberta Carlsson back at the Boston office and asked if there was any update on the hunt for the Cain brothers. She told him that there was not. It was a short call.

Early Simms parked his cruiser across the street and Lowe watched as a woman got out the passenger door. Early looked different when he spoke to her, more relaxed. They smiled and she kissed him before heading in the opposite direction towards the centre of town. Early started across the street. He saw Lowe and raised a hand in greeting.

The bell above the door rang when Early pushed in to the diner. He took off his cap, nodded at Pat and sat opposite Lowe by the window.

'You ordered yet?' he asked Lowe.

Lowe shook his head.

'Who was that?' he asked, nodding to the street outside. 'I mean, the woman that was in your car.'

'Someone I knew a while ago.'

'Looks like you've re-acquainted yourselves.'

A waitress came to their table and they ordered food – Early opting for a toasted BLT and Lowe for a tuna-mayo sandwich.

'So what's going on, Nick?' Early asked when the waitress left their table.

'My wife says I need to apologise before I do anything

else.'

'She sounds like a smart woman.'

'Much smarter than me.'

'I think I'd have to agree with that assessment.'

Lowe smiled.

'I'm sorry, Early.'

'About what?'

'I misled you. Or, at least, I didn't tell you the whole story.'

'Go on.'

'My primary role is on the anti-corruption task force out of the Boston field office. I've been working there for more than a year now.'

Early nodded.

'I guess you figured that out.'

'You're looking at cops?'

'Not just cops, but that's a key focus.'

'Kapnick.'

Lowe put his hands flat on the table and looked outside. The waitress came back with their food order and they sat quietly until she left the table. Early took a bite from his sandwich, waiting for Lowe to continue.

'I can't say anything about that,' Lowe said eventually, starting in on his sandwich.

'How long have you been interested in him?'

'Since the beginning. I mean, when I first got onto the task force. He was already a person of interest.'

'For what?'

Lowe made a face at him.

'You been looking at me too?' Early asked, watching Lowe's reaction closely.

'We have to rule out close associates of the main target.'

'I'll take that as a yes. When was I ruled out?'

'Long time ago. I mean, it was before this thing with the Cains if that's what you're really asking.'

'So what's up with the Cains? Why did you get involved?'

Lowe wiped his mouth with a paper napkin and took a

drink of his Coke.

'I want to be straight with you,' he told Early.

'So, be straight.'

'I didn't need to be on the Cain job. It was Bobbie and Keller. The other agents you met at the house.'

'You tagged along thinking that it was close enough to here that you could flatter me, pull me in and use that as a way of getting closer to my boss.'

'Yes.'

'I appreciate you didn't try to sugar coat the answer.'

'I told you, I want to be straight with you.'

They sat for another few minutes without speaking, finishing off their lunch. Lowe waited for Early to speak.

'Look, I get it,' Early said, 'I really do. But if you cleared me already I would have appreciated a more honest approach.'

'You have to understand how we work on this stuff. I couldn't tell you. We have to keep a tight circle of knowledge. That's all it was.'

'But you're invested in getting these Cain boys now, right? I mean, they're not just a piece of misdirection.'

'I want them.'

68

Kate bought two pairs of lightweight pants, a summer dress and two tops, all from the same shop. She preferred economy of effort when it came to clothes shopping and was happy to find what she needed in a single location. She quickly tried each item on before deciding to buy and paid with her credit card. When she was finished, she got a bottle of water from a store across south of the sheriff's office and stood sipping from it and watching Early talk to the FBI agent at their table by the window in Kennedy's.

It looked like an intense conversation, punctuated by short silences. She felt that there was probably a lot of testosterone involved in the exchange. She found it difficult to judge the behaviour of men but in the end it looked like they came to some kind of agreement.

He was coming into the living room after being out in the back yard when Joe Foley saw John Lustig pause at the bottom of the path leading to the front door of the house. Joe stood still and watched.

Lustig looked bad. His clothes were dishevelled, as if he had not changed them in a few days. His hair was unkempt and sticking up in places and the skin under his eyes was so dark that it looked bruised.

Joe turned and said his wife's name. Bree Foley came to join her husband and looked outside when he pointed through the window. She watched as Lustig remained at the bottom of the path staring up at the front door.

'He looks terrible,' she said. 'Maybe you should go talk to him.'

Joe Foley thought that it could go one of two ways judging by Lustig's appearance: either he was deeply sorry about what had happened and looked like that because he was wracked by guilt; or a switch in his brain had been flicked to the 'off' position. His vacant stare made Joe lean towards the latter interpretation. He considered himself, after a long career as a lawyer, a pretty good judge of people. But he recognised that he had been wrong before.

Lustig started walking up the path and Joe moved to the door, pulling it open when Lustig was still around ten feet away. Lustig stopped when he saw Joe.

'What can I do for you, John?' Joe asked, stepping onto the porch and pulling the door almost closed behind him.

Lustig did not look Joe in the eyes when he spoke.

'I want to see my wife. I want to see Kate.'

'I don't think that's a good idea right now.'

Lustig frowned.

'Are you saying you won't let me see her?'

'It's not within my power to make that decision.'

'Sounds like you think it is.'

Lustig's voice started to rise in volume. Joe felt uncomfortable, looking up and down the street.

'I want to see her, Joe. I want to see her, now.'

He almost shouted the last word. Joe backed up and pushed the door open, putting one foot inside the house. He turned to look for his wife. When he turned back to Lustig, the man was almost at the door and had a gun in his hand.

Lustig was done with the old bastard. He moved quickly up with the path, reached behind his back and pulled the handgun from the waistband of his pants. He took aim at Joe Foley and saw the look of surprise on the man's face. Then he pulled the trigger. He fired twice in quick succession. Foley ducked and tried to move back into the house but both bullets hit him. Lustig saw red blooms on Foley's shirt. The old man fell backwards into the house. He heard a woman scream and walked into the house.

Bree Foley came into the hallway, bending over her husband. She pressed her hands to the wounds on his torso, blood leaking over her hands. Lustig took aim at her. She turned, saw him and raised a bloody hand in front of her face.

Lustig pushed her hand aside, stepped forward and hit her in the face with the gun. He heard a cracking sound and a long gash opened up on Bree's cheek. The wound gaped and started to bleed. Bree's eyes widened in shock but she did not fall. Lustig hit her again, this time sweeping the gun across her forehead opening a ragged cut in her flesh. She fell back against the wall and looked up at Foley, her eyelids fluttering at the edge of consciousness. Lustig put the barrel of the gun under her right eye.

'Kate, if you're here you better come here right now or I'm going to shoot your mother.'

He listened but there was no sound.

'Kate, I swear to Christ I'm going to kill her.'

Bree tried to raise a hand to push the gun from her face but she could not coordinate her movements. Her hand waved ineffectually in the air.

Lustig was aware enough to know that on this quiet street his shooting would shortly cause neighbours to come out and investigate. He looked outside but saw no one there. Bree Foley tried to speak, but the blows to her head caused her words to be indistinct when she spoke.

'Are you saying she's not here?' Lustig asked. 'Cause I can't understand you right now, Bree.'

He pushed the gun hard into her face. She flapped her hand at him, tears streaming down her face.

'Is she here?' Lustig shouted.

Bree managed to shake her head, no.

Lustig stepped into the hall and shouted his wife's name again. He became aware of voices outside and knew that he had to get out of there.

Lustig left the house, walked quickly down the path and towards his car. Someone shouted at him but he ignored it. He knew that his wife must be in town somewhere because her car was here and so she would not have gone far. A dark thought occurred to him: that maybe she was with another man if she had not taken her car.

'Motherfucker better watch out,' he said to himself as he got into his car and pulled away from the kerb.

69

Bree knew that her husband was in trouble. Her head was fuzzy, but she had enough clarity of thought to recognise that he was losing blood and that his breathing was shallow and uneven. She put a hand to his face, streaking his skin with her blood. The initial shock of the event was wearing off and the pain from Bree's own wounds started to throb. Her jaw felt loose and lopsided where Lustig had smashed the gun into her face the first time. She turned her head and a stream of blood slewed from her mouth onto the floor. She put her hands on the floor and tried to push herself up, but her vision darkened and flashes popped in the dark. She did not have the strength and slumped back to the floor.

She heard voices and footsteps outside. Someone screamed nearby. A man's voice said her name repeatedly but she was unable to see who it was.

'Somebody call nine-one-one,' the same man said.

'Is anyone else in the house?' a woman asked. 'What about their daughter, Kate?'

Bree heard Kate's name; knew that Lustig would be looking for her. She wanted to do something, to tell someone. But her injuries overcame her and she passed to unconsciousness.

70

Early waved for Kate to come to the diner when he saw her across the street. She was carrying two bags from a small clothes shop down the street. She looked as good as he could ever remember, her sunglasses mostly hiding the ugly bruising still present around her eyes. Lowe asked watched Kate cross the road.

'Are we still friends?' he asked Early.

'Leave that one with me for now, okay?'

Lowe nodded as the door opened and Kate came into the diner. Early stood and kissed her cheek, taking her bags and letting her sit in his seat. She lifted a napkin from the table and pressed it to her forehead.

'Hot out there,' she said.

Lowe held out his hand and told her who he was.

'I'm Kate,' she said.

'Nice to meet you.'

Early excused himself and went to the restroom at the back of the diner. He was pleased that Lowe had told him the truth, but that just opened up a whole different set of questions: like, what was going to happen to Kapnick and the department? Assuming Lowe was right and Kapnick was dirty.

Lustig turned onto Main Street and slowed the car to less than twenty miles per hour. He leaned forward and looked along both sides of the street, straining to see into shop windows. A guy in a pick-up truck drew up behind him and honked. Lustig ignored the noise.

The street curved gently to the left and as Lustig came around the apex of the bend he saw Kate walking across the street with shopping bags in her hands. He braked sharply and brought the car to a stop. The guy behind him pulled around the stationary car and gave Lustig the finger as he passed. Kate went into a diner on the right-hand side of the street. Lustig could not see inside the diner from his current vantage point. He drove forward until he found a parking space and pulled in. He was twenty feet from the front of the diner. He saw Kate now. She was sitting at a table by the window facing down the street towards him. She was smiling and seemed to be talking to someone on the other side of the table. Lustig was unable to see her companion. He opened the car door and stepped onto the sidewalk, immediately feeling the heat of the sun on his head. He squinted in the bright light, reaching around to make sure that his gun was in place. He closed the car door and walked towards the diner.

Early washed his hands and pulled a hand towel from the dispenser beside the sink. He dried his hands and looked in the mirror, straightening the nametag pinned to the right breast pocket of his shirt. His radio crackled to life.

'All officers,' Shirley Lee's voice sounded, 'please proceed to Oyster Road. Multiple reports of shots fired. Proceed with caution.'

Early keyed the send button on his mike, turning his head to speak into the device clipped to his shirt.

'What's the address, Shirley?'

'Uh, I don't have that at the moment. Are you able to respond?'

'Copy that. I'm on my way. I can be there in a few minutes.'

Early pulled open the restroom door, hoping that it was a coincidence that a shooting had taken place on the street where Joe and Bree Foley lived.

Kate's eyes flicked up to the face of the man that walked past the window. Lowe saw her smile falter and then she turned sharply in her seat as the same man came into the diner.

'John…' Kate said, starting to rise out of her seat.

Lowe saw the fear in Kate's face before she turned to the man. He heard the same fear in her voice when she said his name.

The man ignored Kate and looked at Lowe.

'Who's this fucking guy?' he asked.

'John…'

Early came out of the restroom and saw the man come into the diner at the same time as Kate turned to face him. He heard Kate say her husband's name. The place was almost full with lunchtime trade, most of who turned to see what the commotion was. Early's hand went to his weapon, instinct kicking in.

John Lustig took a gun from the waistband of his jeans, swung it around and aimed at Nick Lowe. Kate stepped back and put her hands out in front of her. One of the waitresses screamed. Lowe started to stand, his hand going inside his jacket for his own weapon.

Lustig shot Lowe three times almost point blank. Lowe toppled backwards over his chair, blood spattering the window.

Kate flinched as some of Lowe's blood spotted her face.

Early moved forward. He pulled his weapon free of its holster. A man stood up from his seat directly in Early's line of sight. Early put his shoulder full force into the man, sending him sprawling over the top of a table and then head first onto the floor.

Lustig looked at Early and then back at Kate. He moved the gun towards her and fired again. Kate tried to grab the gun as it swung her way. She missed and Lustig fired again.

Early saw Kate's white blouse puff outwards, gunshot residue from Lustig's weapon smudging it black. She fell against the window, her hand clutching at her side as blood started to pour from the wound.

Early brought his weapon up and planted his feet. It was chaos all around him as people screamed and fell to the floor. He took aim at Lustig and fired.

Early's first two shots missed. Lustig pulled the trigger of his gun again as the second of Early's bullets hit the frame of the door, inches from Lustig's face. Splinters dug into his cheek, causing him to flinch as he discharged his weapon at Kate.

The bullet hit Kate high, breaking her collarbone. The impact with the bone deflected the trajectory of the bullet upwards where it tore out through the top of Kate's shoulder and shattered the window behind her.

Kate's knees buckled and she fell.

Lustig swivelled towards Early.

Early fired twice more. Both shots found their target. The first clipped Lustig's chin before entering his throat. The second went through his left eye and killed him instantly.

Lustig's head snapped back. His legs went out from under him and he fell straight to the floor.

71

Kate was breathing rapidly when Early reached her. Her face was pale and damp from sweat. The floor underfoot was slick with blood. Early was aware of the chaos behind him. He put a hand on Kate's cheek and told her to hold on.

Early turned and shouted Pat Kennedy's name, his eyes searching the diner for the man. Pat stood up from behind the counter. His eyes were wide.

'Get everyone out the back door,' Early told him. 'Get them out now, Pat.'

Kennedy nodded at him and came around the counter shouting for everyone to move to the back. He had to shout to be heard over the screams and sobs.

Early turned back to Kate.

'You'll be okay,' he told her.

She nodded, blood soaking her blouse from both wounds.

'Try to breathe more normally,' Early said.

He did not think that she really knew what was happening. He looked behind her at Nick Lowe and saw his eyes staring emptily at the ceiling above him.

Someone shouted Early's name from outside. He looked across the street through the broken window and saw Henry Kapnick and Frank Wood standing on the steps of the sheriff's building. He raised a hand and waved them over.

'We need an ambulance over here,' he roared at them.

Kate said his name. He looked at her.

'He shot me,' she said. 'John shot me.'

She squeezed her eyes shut and tears ran down her cheeks.

'You're gonna make it,' Early to her. 'Hold on now.'

Kapnick came into the diner and looked at Early crouching beside Kate. Blood had soaked into Early's pants where he kneeled on the floor.

'Holy shit…' Frank Wood said as he came in behind Kapnick.

'Frank,' Kapnick said to his youngest deputy, 'go out back and help Pat with those people.'

He pointed to the rear of the diner where the last of the remaining customers were pushing at each other to get out. Wood nodded and ran to the back of the diner.

Early looked up at Kapnick and saw his boss looking at Nick Lowe's body. Kapnick's face was difficult to read.

'Oyster Road,' Early said.

Kapnick frowned.

'What?'

'There was a report of shots fired on Oyster Road. That's where Kate's parents live.'

Kapnick keyed his mike and told his other deputy, Randy Jones, to get over to Oyster Road.

'What the hell happened here?' Kapnick asked.

Early shook his head and turned back to Kate. Her eyes were shut and her breathing was laboured.

'You got an ambulance on the way?' Early asked.

Kapnick said that he had.

'We need it here now.'

Kapnick put a hand on Early's shoulder and told him that he knew that.

Early strained to hear the sound of a siren, but there was none.

72

They had no money left and Jimmy could tell that Marshall was approaching the limit of his tolerance for being stuck all day in the motel room. His brother was restless and agitated, flicking between TV channels and pacing the length of the room. He spoke frequently and at length but not always coherently. Most of it sounded like he was arguing with himself but was largely inaudible to Jimmy.

Jimmy knew well enough that they could not evade the law forever. But he was determined to keep his head down as long as he could to let the heat go out of the situation. The cops always had the next killing to deal with and the old ones faded and were forgotten in time.

Trouble was, you needed cash or credit eventually and that's when they would nail you. It was a problem. The only solution Jimmy could come up with was to get some money from a non-legal source. That would mean going out again in public and putting himself at risk. He had been monitoring all the local news channels and it seemed like either he and Marshall had not been linked to the deaths at the house as yet or the cops were keeping their names and pictures off of the news for now. Some of the reporters talked about the 'extreme levels of violence' perpetrated on the victims and how the police were anxious to apprehend those responsible. It was never any more specific than that.

'We need money,' Jimmy told Marshall as his brother came out of the bathroom, pulling up the zipper on his jeans. 'I don't have anything left.'

Marshall looked at him for a moment then lay on his bed with his arms crossed over his face.

'I'm going fucking crazy in here, Jimmy. I just about can't take it any more, you know.'

'I know.'

Marshall sat upright.

'So let's go,' he said. 'Back to Boston. They ain't looking for us bro'. We'd have been on the news if they were. Nobody knows it was us.'

Jimmy knew that his brother believed what he said. He had such a black and white view of the world. It would not have occurred to him that there might be a reason for their identities to be held back by the cops.

'We have to be smart and stay careful,' Jimmy said.

Marshall flopped back on the bed and punched the wall at his head. He hit it hard enough to make a small dent in the drywall.

'I need to go get some money while you wait here.'

Marshall was about to protest again but stopped. If Jimmy was going to leave him alone again it would give him a chance to see the girl. Maybe even do more than see her.

'I'll wait till it gets dark,' Jimmy said.

73

'You have to stay here and do your job,' Henry Kapnick told Early, placing a hand on the bigger man's chest.

Early had indicated a strong desire to follow the ambulance taking Kate to the hospital. He clenched his fists by his side then released them as the vehicle pulled away from outside the diner, a single blare of its siren alerting other road users to get out of the way.

'You shot that man,' Kapnick said, inclining his head to the prone figure of John Lustig. 'That has to be written up.'

Early was standing at the counter in Kennedy's diner, his pants soaked in blood and streaks of it on showing on his face. Early put a hand to his forehead and ran it up over his head. He nodded at Kapnick.

'The other Feds will be here in…'

Kapnick looked at his watch.

'Maybe fifty minutes. They're on the way from Boston.'

Early watched Frank Wood try to maintain control outside of the crowd had formed outside. People peered into the building from behind the crime scene tape that had been used to keep the sidewalk immediately outside the diner clear of anyone that might get in the way. Cars slowed as they passed the scene, rubberneckers trying to get a glimpse of the carnage.

It had been less than an hour since Early shot Lustig to death and Early realised now that he had not heard what had happened on Oyster Road. Randy Jones had not appeared at the diner as yet.

'You heard from Randy?' Early asked Kapnick.

The sheriff rubbed at his chin and looked outside.

'I did.'

'And?'

'Joe Foley got shot. He's in a bad way.'

'What about Bree?' Early asked.

'She got beat up. Bad but not life threatening. There's another rig over there now.'

Early's mouth felt thick with saliva. He wanted to shoot Lustig again so as to release some of the rage building in him.

'Take a moment, Early,' Kapnick said, reading his deputy's eyes and putting a hand on Early's upper arm. 'Sit down and have a drink of water or something.'

Early sat back on the nearest stool by the counter. He put a hand on the counter edge and gripped it hard, expecting to break a chunk off in his hand.

Kapnick watched him closely.

'I need to go help Frank,' Kapnick said. 'Can I leave you alone here?'

'Go help Frank.'

74

The Massachusetts Office of the Chief Medical Examiner did not have a satellite facility for conducting autopsies on-Cape between 2002 and 2012, when the new facility at the edge of Sandwich opened for its grim business. The new facility, which cost north of five million dollars to construct, was a boon for the law enforcement agencies on the Cape.

The previous facility, at the old Pocasset County Hospital, had gotten so bad before it closed that the Massachusetts office could not achieve the appropriate accreditation with the National Association of Chief Medical Examiners. State budgets being what they were, it took the best part of ten years to get the new facility built. The absence of a facility on the island had meant that officers from the Cape had to travel to Boston for autopsies in criminal cases. The local ME, Arnett Bain, had transferred from the Boston facility when the new one on the Cape opened. He was a native of the island and jumped at the chance to come home.

The ME's van pulled up outside the diner not long after the ambulance left to take Kate to the hospital. Early did not know Bain well, but had been impressed by his professionalism on each occasion when he had attended on scene with the man. Bain was slim, with round, frameless glasses and close cropped hair. He stepped down from the cab of the van wearing beige chinos and a white shirt with the sleeves rolled up to his elbows. The ME's van was white and bore subtle livery, trying to avoid announcing the nature of its cargo too loudly. The cops on the Cape had taken to calling it 'the Bucket'. Bain did not openly express a view on the nickname, but secretly he enjoyed it. He was a man with a dry sense of humour. That was almost a pre-requisite for his particular vocation.

Bain came into the diner while his assistant stayed outside. He looked at the bodies of the two men lying on the floor and then at Early.

'You know these men?'

Early nodded.

'One of them is an FBI agent from out of Boston.'

Bain looked at the bodies again and said, 'Shit.'

'The one in the suit and tie?'

Early said yes and told Bain Lowe's name.

'You done with them yet?'

'No. There are federal agents on their way from Boston. You can't take them until they clear the scene.'

Bain walked to the counter and sat on a stool next to Early.

'You don't look too good, deputy. Are you okay?'

Early shook his head and then nodded.

'Yeah. I don't know.'

'You were close to the agent?'

'Close enough.'

Bain nodded.

'What happened?' he asked.

Early rubbed a hand over his mouth. He pointed at Lustig and told Bain what he could remember, though it seemed distant and fragmented in his mind. He did not mention his connection to Kate. Bain shook his head when Early finished.

'I heard on the radio on the way here about some kerfuffle over on Oyster Road. The same guy responsible for that too?'

Early said that was what they thought.

'What is it with people?' Bain asked.
Early had no answer to his question.

Kapnick had Shirley Lee bring them all coffees from a drive-thru Starbucks not far from the centre of town. Early could not bear to be in the diner any longer with Nick Lowe's body on the floor so he drank his outside on the sidewalk with Frank Wood while waiting for the FBI agents to arrive. Bain and his assistant kept themselves busy with whatever equipment they had in the back of the Bucket. The sun dipped behind a low cloudbank and a light breeze lifted the oppressive heat of the day.

Agents Carlsson and Parrish eventually arrived in their standard issue dark coloured sedan. They parked behind the Bucket. Early waited for them and took them into the diner and went through it all again. Carlsson made him walk through his movements, describing the scene as he went. It helped somehow distance Early from the events, as if for a time he was no more than an observer rather than a participant. She took notes as Early recounted his story and also recorded him on a digital recording device no larger than a cell phone. Parrish sketched out the scene in a notebook and took over a hundred photographs with a professional standard camera. Early told him that they had already done that, but Parrish said that he wanted his own record.

Early went outside with Carlsson while Parrish continued documenting the scene.

'How well did you know Agent Lowe?' he asked Carlsson.

She looked inside the diner, as if trying to locate her fellow agent to see if that would help her remember.

'Uh, not well. I mean we were not on the same team.'

'It's okay,' Early told her, 'I know why he was really here.'

'He told you?'

'Yes.'

Parrish came out of the diner and went to the Bureau car

to store the results of his efforts.

'You heard any more about the Cain brothers?' Early asked.

She shook her head.

'We'll catch them. They can't stay gone forever.'

'They won't come quietly.'

'I think you're probably right about that.'

Parrish told the ME that the bodies were cleared for removal and came to stand beside Early and Carlsson. They watched in silence as Bain and his assistant went about their task of loading the bodies into the van.

75

The deputies' room at the sheriff's office felt small and cramped with five people in it – the three deputies and two FBI agents. The agents alternatively stood or sat on spare seats while talking animatedly into their cell phones. Early blocked out the noise and concentrated on his own work. He had called the hospital and told them to let him know immediately there was any news on Kate. All he knew so far was that she had been in surgery for more than four hours. He did not have a status update on either of her parents.

Early was not certain if Kapnick had made it plain to the agents that he did not want them in his room or if they were simply avoiding him given the Bureau's ongoing investigation into the man. Early still had no idea what his boss was into.

It seemed clear enough that Lustig had gone looking for Kate at her parents' place before finding her in town. If the sum total of his endeavours turned out to be one dead body then, Early supposed, they had gotten off lightly. It could have been much worse.

Lustig was the first person that Early had killed on duty. In fact, it was the first occasion on which Early had required to draw and discharge his weapon other than at the practice range. All of the weapons training instructors he had worked with in law enforcement had told him the same thing: that it would be different firing upon another human being than it would be at targets on a range. Truth was, Early had not found it so different. Sure, it was more chaotic with people running and screaming and getting in the way. But the same principles applied: find your target and engage. He was frustrated to have missed with both of his first shots, but he had had to deal with the guy that got in his way and the danger that Lustig posed to Kate had caused him to snatch at the trigger. He didn't make any mistake with the second volley.

He typed his report on screen in sparse, succinct language. They had the perpetrator of the crime and there would be no need for an extended investigation or prosecution. It was, in law enforcement terms, neat and easily compartmentalised. When he finished, he e-mailed the report to Kapnick. He rose from his seat and walked down the corridor to the sheriff's room, knocking on the door before pushing it open. Kapnick was on his cell phone and held up a hand to indicate to Early that he was to wait until the call was finished. Early stood in the doorway.

'I said that, already,' Kapnick told the person on the other end of the call. 'I mean, what else do you need me to say. It's done.'

It was fairly standard Kappy charm. The sheriff turned to face away from Early and listened without speaking for a moment.

'It doesn't matter to me any longer. Do what you want with it. Keep it or don't keep it.'

Kapnick listened some more, grunted a terse, 'goodbye' and ended the call.

'Some fucking people,' he said to Early, dropping the phone onto his desk and shaking his head. 'Are those Feds still here?'

Early said that they were.

'What else do they need tonight, huh? I mean, I know the guy was one of theirs, but it's not exactly a whodunit.'

'They have procedures they need to follow.'

Kapnick leaned back in his chair and rolled his neck. Early waited for his boss.

'Tough day,' Kapnick said eventually, clasping his hands on the desk and looking at Early. 'That agent was a friend of yours.'

Early nodded.

'And the girl too,' Kapnick added.

Early did not want to get into it with him right now.

'Did you get my report? I emailed it to you.'

Kapnick did not look at his computer screen.

'I'm going to the hospital now. To see how Kate is doing.'

He knew that not asking for permission would rile Kapnick in a small way but did not care. Kapnick did not react outwardly.

76

The pain in Manu Polite's head was all consuming. After his call with Kapnick, when he discovered that the FBI agent had been killed, he lay back on his bed with the blinds closed and all lights off. It didn't help. His jaw throbbed and it felt like his head would burst open. Sweat formed quickly on his forehead and ran into his hair. After a few minutes, he wrenched himself from the bed and went to the bathroom. The light made his head hurt more.

Polite knew when he looked in the mirror that he had more to worry about than a broken jaw. The whole side of his face was swollen and red. He figured that he must have an infection. He leaned over the sink and spat a mixture of blood and something else into the sink. The sight of it made him dry heave. He quickly turned the water on and rinsed it away.

The gun that Kapnick had told him to get rid of was sitting on the floor beside his bed. Polite kneeled by the bed and lifted the gun. It felt heavier than it had previously. He cocked the hammer and held the barrel of the weapon against his temple, wondering what it would be like to pull the trigger and end his pain. It was not a life that he would greatly regret leaving behind. He sat like that for a minute, not sure how serious he was about doing it.

He eased the hammer back down while depressing the trigger and let the gun fall into his lap. He was not sure if he had not done it because he was not yet ready to die or out of cowardice.

He had travelled a long way from the islands, but it occurred to him that he had not come very far at all.

77

The Blackwater hospital is a modern, two-storey building in red brick with one of the most renowned emergency departments in the state. It shares its hilltop campus to the northwest of the town with the local VNA facility and a medical office complex. It is not a large facility by national standards – with around ninety beds – but it had upgraded steadily over the last twenty years and Early felt confident that Kate would get the best care available there. The paramedics had treated her at the diner, pushing fluids and stabilising her vital signs before deciding to transport her to the hospital. He hoped that the immediate emergency care that she had received gave her a good chance at surviving her injuries.

The first wound that Lustig had inflicted, low on her abdomen, was what concerned Early the most. If it had hit a major organ or artery then she would be in trouble. The second wound, while painful, was eminently survivable with only tissue and bone damage.

Early found a parking space close to the main entrance and walked quickly to the doors. He showed the staff at reception his identification and asked about the Foley family. He was told that Kate was out of surgery and in the intensive care unit but was unconscious and he would not be permitted to see her at this time. Her father was still in surgery.

'What about Mrs Foley?' he asked.

'She's in a room on the first floor. If you want to wait for a second I can have someone take you to her.'

Early said that he would wait but that he wanted to speak to the surgeon who had operated on Kate.

'I'll see what I can do about that,' the receptionist told him.

Early turned off his cell phone to comply with a sign at the desk and sat on a plastic chair in a small waiting area. An older woman was there with a man who looked like her son. Early nodded at them but got no reaction. Maybe it was the uniform.

Clinical staff passed by as he sat waiting. Some of them laughed with each other, talking about something that someone had said or what they had seen on TV last night. Others looked serious while flipping through official looking papers. Early had never been the brightest academic star, preferring to major in sports. But he was not a man that felt ill at ease with his abilities. He related to medical staff as fellow professionals and if he did not understand any particular jargon he said so and asked for a simple explanation. There was no point, he felt, in pretending to understand something that you did not just to seem smarter. That was a pretty stupid approach to life.

It was almost seven in the evening and the sun was sinking slowly, the sky darkening to a deeper shade of blue. Early liked this time of the day. It reminded him of the days he spent with his dad working on the cabin and sitting in the back yard with a beer after the physical labour of the day was done. They talked about sports and the job and otherwise enjoyed the peace that twilight brought. There was little or no traffic noise at that time, with birdcalls and the buzz of insects almost seeming amplified in the quiet.

He recalled one conversation in particular. It was probably the last exchange they had before Early noticed his dad's memory lapses starting to become pronounced and out of the ordinary.

'You like the job, Early?' Charlie Simms had asked his

son. 'Not everyone is cut out for it, you know.'

'I like it.'

'You can deal with the rough and tumble of it, no doubt. But what about the boredom when all you got is reports to write and bureaucracy to deal with?'

Early took a long drink from his beer and watched a bird settle in the upper branches of a tree by the pond, its head darting from side to side.

'I like people, you know,' Early said, still watching the bird. 'I mean, I know we get to see their bad side, but that's part of life.'

'You think maybe you can help them, is that it?'

'I know better than that, Dad. Some of them are just bad and nothing I can do is going to change that. That type of man, and it is mostly men, need the…what did you call it?'

'Rough and tumble?'

Early laughed. He remembered looking at his dad as a wide grin crinkled the old man's face.

'I can deal with the rough and tumble,' Early said.

His father finished his beer and held the bottle up. Early nodded, indicating that he was ready for another. His father went into the kitchen, which was now almost finished, and Early heard him opening the fridge door and popping the caps off of two bottles. His father came up behind Early's chair and handed him the new bottle, condensation making it slick in his grasp.

'I never told you enough how proud I was of you out on that football field, son,' his father said from behind Early. 'You were a force, by god. Ain't never seen anyone like you.'

His dad put a hand on his shoulder and squeezed it.

'You'll be a fine cop too. I know it.'

'I'll do my best, Dad.'

'That's all anyone can ever ask of you, Early.'

A surgeon in blue scrubs came into the waiting area and introduced himself to Early as Doctor Lee. He was an Asian man and more than half a foot shorter than Early. He had the physical presence that Early associated with good surgeons – stocky with strong forearms and hands.

'You asked about the Foley family, deputy?'

Early nodded and stood.

'How are they doing?'

'Well, surgery went as well as it could on Miss Foley. She's sedated and in ICU at the moment.'

'What was the extent of her injuries?'

Early was surprised at how even his voice sounded.

'She lost a lot of blood but everything major was intact. I'm cautiously optimistic.'

'That's good. What about Joe?'

'I don't know about him, I'm sorry. I understood that you wanted to speak to Mrs Foley?'

Early said that he did and followed Lee around several corners and down short hallways. It seemed to Early that all hospitals were built the same way: a maze designed by some lunatic.

They eventually stopped at a door that Lee gently knocked on and pushed open. Bree Foley was sitting up with pillows propped at her back. She half-turned her head and looked at Early as he came into the room. Her face was badly swollen and discoloured with heavy bandaging. Crusted blood still clung to her skin in small patches.

Lee did not enter the room. He closed the door as Early sat on the chair by the bed.

'How are you, Mrs Foley?'

'Everything hurts.'

She tried to smile but it didn't work. She closed her eyes and tears leaked onto her cheeks. Early took a tissue from a box beside on the table by the bed and dabbed at her cheeks.

'You have a strong family. I'm sure that everyone will make it through this.'

She inclined her head slightly, gritting her teeth while she talked.

'Thank you for saying that, Early.'

'I'll be here for all of you if you need me.'

'Did you arrest the man that did this to us?'

'No, Ma'am, I did not. I shot him dead.'

Bree turned her head further to try to face him. He could see the pain that it caused her.

'I don't know how to feel about that,' she said.

'If I had been given the opportunity to arrest him I would have done.'

'Did you kill him because he hurt Kate?'

'No. I did it because he was going to hurt her some more. And maybe me too. He had already killed a federal agent and it didn't look like he was going to stop till we were all dead.'

Bree faced forward.

'They said it'll be a while before they know if Joe will make it. Before they know if he'll live.'

'I'm sorry to hear that.'

'Did they tell you about Kate?'

'I just spoke to the doctor. He thinks she'll be okay.'

'That's something, then, isn't it?'

Early said that it was. He stood and said that he had to go. Bree Foley reached out and grabbed his wrist. Her grip was strong in spite of her injuries.

'I'm glad it was him and not you, Early. For the sake of my daughter.'

'I don't know how this is all going to play out.'

'No one does, son.'

78

Lee was waiting for Early in the hallway.

'Can I look in on Kate Foley?' Early asked.

Lee shook his head.

'I don't need to be in the room. But I would like to see her.'

Lee put his hands on his hips.

'Do you have more than a professional interest in her wellbeing?'

'Yes.'

The surgeon rubbed at faint stubble on the underside of his chin.

'There's no way to see her except to be in her room,' he said. 'It's not about upsetting her, you know. She's unconscious anyway. We control access to limit the chance of infection. Her body has enough trauma to deal with right now and needs time to recover.'

'You're right. I understand.'

Early held out his hand. Lee grasped it and shook firmly.

'Thank you for looking after her, doctor. She means a lot to me.'

'I can see that. She'll get the very best care here, deputy. You can count on that.'

'Will you call me when I can see her?' Early asked, taking a card from his shirt pocket with his name and contact details on it.

Lee took the card and said that he would have someone

call. He offered to walk Early to the exit.

'I heard what you said in there,' Lee told him as they walked. 'About shooting the man that did this.'

Early waited for Lee to ask his next question.

'As a doctor, I'm curious. I mean I spend my time trying to hold back death. But you…'

'What?'

'I don't mean to offend you, deputy.'

'You're not. What is it that you want to know, doctor?'

'How does it feel when you first shoot and kill a person? I'm interested from a clinical perspective.'

Early stopped walking and turned to face Lee.

'I only ever killed that one man. Truth is that he deserved to die in that moment. I don't have any problem in telling you that. It's my job to protect others from people like him. But I have no idea how I feel about it. Right now I'm trying to deal with the feelings I have for his victims.'

'I'm sorry. I didn't…'

'I'm not angry, doctor. I don't even know what I feel. Ask me about it when Kate wakes up.'

They continued to the exit in silence and shook hands again when they got there.

Early went to his car, closed the door and stared at the hospital building as the sky darkened. He thought about the lie he had told Doctor Lee. John Lustig was not the first person he had killed.

79

The house that Henry Kapnick inherited when his mother died was a modest two-storey affair near Silver Pond, about halfway between East Blackwater and his office on Main Street. It was a quiet street with houses owned by families mostly. The front yards were small and neat.

It was almost fully dark when Kapnick slowed and pulled into the short driveway in front of his house. It had been a day that he had not experienced before as sheriff and he was glad that it was over. It was a difficult day for the town and for the Foley family in particular. He had his fair share of head butting with Joe Foley in the past when Joe had defended criminals arrested by Kapnick or his deputies, but he did not wish the man any ill.

Kapnick knew that the death of Nick Lowe was not the end of his troubles with the FBI, but it felt like an important moment. Lowe, he was aware, had been leading the inquiry aimed at him. It might at least give him a little breathing space. Maybe even enough time to retire and buy a place somewhere far away from here. He had often thought about somewhere on the west coast. San Diego looked like a place he would enjoy.

He was thinking about a small beach-front property as he walked to his front door and put the key into the lock. He did not see Manu Polite step around the corner of the house until it was too late.

Kapnick turned his head when he saw movement close to

him.

Polite raised his arm and pointed the gun at Kapnick's face.

Kapnick jerked his head back and put a hand up, as if that alone would ward off death.

Polite shot him three times. The first bullet hit Kapnick's hand and was deflected down into his bicep where it came to rest. The other two hit him in the face, one of them shattering his jaw and exiting just in front of his right ear. The final bullet entered his left cheek before going through his mouth and out the back of his neck. None of the wounds was immediately fatal, but the damage was catastrophic.

Kapnick fell against his door and went to the ground. Blood poured from his wounds and soaked his shirt. He felt his mouth and throat fill with blood, choking off his air supply. He coughed and sprayed blood.

Polite looked around to see if anyone had seen him. The street was empty.

Kapnick grabbed at the gun in his holster, pulling it free as Polite looked away. He found it difficult to focus but knew that he had to return fire immediately. He pulled the trigger repeatedly as he brought the gun to bear, only really aware of Polite as a dark outline against the light from the streetlamps.

Polite flinched at the sound of the first shot, which went wide to his left. He turned as Kapnick kept shooting, feeling something hot tugging at his thigh and groin. He fell and rolled away as Kapnick kept shooting until his magazine was empty.

Polite knew that he had taken probably two rounds. He got up and stumbled forward before falling on Kapnick's driveway. He was aware of the sounds of people's voices. He tried to stand again but his muscles would not respond. He crawled to Kapnick's car and sat with his back against the fender. He looked at his leg, his hands searching in the dark for the wound. He found it and felt blood pulse freely from his severed femoral artery over his hands and onto the ground. Polite did not know it, but he was only a few minutes from death.

Kapnick watched Polite flailing around and coming to rest at his car. He saw the pool of blood forming quickly on the ground below the man. He tried to laugh, but only managed to gargle the blood that had filled his throat and was now seeping into his lungs to suffocate him.

80

He pushed a full magazine into the handle of the gun that he had taken from the bedroom of the Applegate family. Jimmy Cain looked at the other two magazines at the bottom of the bag. He picked them up and put one in each of the back pockets of his jeans. He figured that it would be better to have them with him in case he was unable to come back to the motel. It was a thought that he did not express to Marshall. He knew that his brother would be unlikely to stay in the room if he thought that he would end up alone there.

Jimmy went to the window while Marshall flicked TV channels between a wrestling match and a movie starring Sandra Bullock that Jimmy had not seen before. He pulled the curtains open a little and looked out into the parking lot. He could hear noise from the McDonald's restaurant, kids talking loud and laughing, but otherwise it was quiet out there.

'I'm going out now, Marshall.'

Jimmy turned from the window. Marshall appeared to ignore him, staring intently at the TV. Ignoring him was something Marshall did when he had a secret, Jimmy knew. His brother thought that by saying nothing he was being smart. In reality, he was telling Jimmy everything.

Jimmy sat on Marshall's bed.

'What's up, buddy?' he asked.

He could see the effort of continuing to ignore him showing in Marshall's face. Jimmy smiled thinly. His brother looked like he did as a young kid and it reminded Jimmy of better times, of the apartment building where they used to live and the old lady that smelled of talcum powder and cinnamon.

'I'll get us some money and then we can get out of here. Go somewhere new, you know. You want to go somewhere new?'

Marshall's eyes flicked to his brother and a look of concern passed across his features, his mouth tightening and a frown creasing his brow. Jimmy wondered what it was about this place that made Marshall want to stay, if that's what the look meant.

'Listen,' Jimmy said. 'Don't worry. We'll talk about it when I get back.'

He stood and put a hand on top of Marshall's head, feeling the heat of his brother's skin. Jimmy leaned down and kissed Marshall's head.

'Keep that door locked. Don't answer unless it's me that comes knocking.'

It was pleasantly warm outside. Jimmy walked across the parking lot, looking back at the room a couple of times, a little unsettled by Marshall's mood. He reached the far side of the parking lot, leading out onto the street. The McDonald's across the road was busy. A group of skater kids were messing around noisily outside. Jimmy watched them for a moment, wondering what it felt like to be that careless of the world around you. As he watched them, a police cruiser pulled into the lot of the restaurant and two local cops stepped out. One of them looked across the road at Jimmy. He realised that he must look weird standing there staring at the kids. He moved immediately to his right, walking at a steady pace and not looking back at the cop. He turned right at the next junction, out of view of the cops, expecting the cruiser to follow him around the corner. He stopped, leaned against the wall and reached around to grasp the gun tucked into his jeans. The cop car did not show.

Jimmy looked along the street and saw a bar not far away and a convenience store at the next corner. He did not want to do anything with those cops nearby. He walked to the bar and pushed the door open, figuring that he would get a beer to pass the time with his last couple of dollars.

Marshall counted slowly to ten a number of times after Jimmy had left the room until he lost track. He got up from the bed and went to the window. He could not see Jimmy in the parking lot. He went to the bathroom and wet his hands with water, pushing his hair back from his face and pressing down on it to keep it in place. He leaned close to the mirror and looked at his face, trying to work out if he looked anything like Jimmy. The girl at the motel reception appeared to like his brother.

Marshall had never been sure what it was that girls liked about men, but whatever it was it sure seemed that Jimmy had it. His brother always got a girl if he wanted to. Marshall had thought that the Chalk girl liked him, the way she put her hands on him in the car that night. He had liked that. But she spoiled it by running and then Jimmy shot her. He didn't feel like Jimmy had to do that. They had taken care of the family in the house and could have taken the girl back to the car. She would have gone with them.

Maybe that was what he had to do, Marshall thought. If he showed that girl that he was not to be fucked with, she would have to do what he wanted.

He went to the main part of the room and opened the gun bag, lifting the shotgun from it. He checked to make sure it was loaded. He stood erect and held the gun in front of his chest. He felt self-conscious and knew that he could not go to the girl like that. He put the gun back in the bag.

Jimmy drank his beer slowly while sitting at a stool by the bar. The place was for serious drinkers, men and women of a certain age that had given up on life. That was fine by Jimmy. He was anonymous in there. He finished the beer after twenty minutes and left the place, walking back to the junction and looking along the street at the McDonald's. The police cruiser was gone.

Jimmy turned and headed for the convenience store. He stopped at the corner opposite the store. It was a small, brightly lit place with what looked like two employees. One of them was behind the counter and the other was re-stocking the shelves. Jimmy leaned against the wall and watched customers come and go for a few minutes. It seemed like a busy place.

Two girls walked past, one of them glancing at Jimmy and smiling. Jimmy was struck by how normal it all felt: having a beer and hanging out on the street corner. He enjoyed watching life go by and for the briefest of instants he forgot about everything. Then the cop car came past the corner, the cop nearest him looking out of his window at Jimmy. He held the cop's gaze until the car rumbled past.

The convenience store wasn't a good bet, Jimmy decided. There were too many people around and he didn't want to get in a situation of trying to control more than one person. This had to be quick and clean. Jimmy was not a man prone to panic, but he felt a sensation in his stomach that he was not accustomed to and drew in a deep breath to combat it.

There was another option, he knew. Walk away. Leave Marshall in the motel and just go. It didn't matter where, so long as it was out of state. He had thought about it more than once since they had been at the motel – that maybe now was the time to let his brother really fend for himself. But he knew that what he would really be doing was abandoning Marshall to the cops, to take the blame for all that they had done. For all of his character flaws, a lack of loyalty was not something that afflicted Jimmy Cain.

A man walked past Jimmy with a baseball cap pulled low on his head and a cigarette dangling from his mouth. Jimmy watched him as he went on down the street past the convenience store before stopping and turning to face the wall. Jimmy saw that there was an ATM sign. He came off the wall, pulled the gun from his jeans and walked quickly to the man. When he reached the ATM he pushed hard against the man and dug the gun into the soft part of his lower back. The man grunted tried to push back, turning his head to see who it was that had pushed into him.

'I got a gun in your back, motherfucker,' Jimmy said in a low voice. 'Move and I'll kill you.'

It had the desired effect. The man froze. Jimmy looked at the screen of the ATM and saw that the man had already chosen the option to withdraw cash.

'Take out three hundred dollars now.'

The man did not move.

'You got two seconds before I do you,' Jimmy said.

The man fumbled at the keypad. The machine whirred and clicked as it counted the money.

'Don't do it, man,' the guy said.

Jimmy looked around. Two cars passed by but no one looked their way; just two buddies at an ATM.

The money slid out. Jimmy reached forward and grabbed it with his free hand, stuffing it in the pocket of his jeans. He stepped back from the man, who closed his eyes and pressed himself closer to the machine.

'Don't turn around. I'll watch you all the way. You look at me once, I'll chase you down and shoot you dead.'

The guy nodded and made a noise like he had intended to say yes but all that came out was a high-pitched whine. Jimmy backed away, then turned and walked away. He looked back three times before reaching the junction at the end of the street. The guy stayed put the whole way.

Jimmy turned the corner and jogged back towards the motel, feeling sweat soak his shirt under the arms.

81

Early pulled up in front of his house and picked up his cell phone from the passenger seat. He had not noticed until now that he had forgotten to turn it on after leaving the hospital. He went into the cabin and saw the light blinking on his landline indicating that he had messages waiting. He pressed 'play' on the answer phone. There were three messages from Frank Wood asking Early to call him, each getting more desperate in tone. Early picked up the phone and called Wood's cell.

'Early, thank fuck it's you,' Wood said when he answered. 'Jesus.'

He sounded out of breath and Early could hear what he thought was crowd noise in the background.

'Frank, it's late. What's this about?'

'It's Kappy.'

Early did not like the young deputy's use of the sheriff's nickname and was about to reprimand him when Wood spoke again.

'He's dead. Manu Polite shot and killed him at his house.'

To that point, Early had not thought that the day could have gotten any worse.

'Where are you, Frank?'

'I'm at the house. At Kappy's. Shit, man, you better get over here. It's just me and Randy. You're the senior guy now.'

'What about Polite?'

'He's here.'

'You have him in custody?'

'He's dead too. It's a mess, Early.'

'I'm coming over.'

Early hung up and ran out the door.

Early turned onto the street where Henry Kapnick had lived until that night and accelerated towards the crowd of people spilling onto the street. Wood's car was parked across the entrance to the driveway with its light bar still flashing red then blue. There was an ambulance parked in front of Wood's car. Early saw that the other deputies had put a cordon around the house, using streetlights to secure yellow police tape in place. Early turned on his own lights as he neared the house and gave a quick blast of his siren. The crowd of onlookers turned and parted as he drove at them, forcing them further back from the house. He stopped and got out, seeing Frank Wood by the front door with a body slumped in a large pool of blood. Two paramedics stood by their rig, one of them smoking. He did not see Randy Jones.

'You people go on back to your homes, now,' Early said, turning and walking towards the crowd of people. 'Let us do our job here.'

They quickly dispersed back to their houses along the street as Early moved towards them. He knew that they would be watching from the safety of their living rooms. Death was always fascinating when it wasn't about you or yours.

Early turned and walked towards the house when the last of the crowd was gone. He saw Jones stand up from behind the sheriff's car and as he walked past the car he saw Polite's body resting against the front fender.

'What happened?' he asked Jones.

'Paramedics say Polite got unlucky,' Wood said, walking towards Early. 'The sheriff got him in the thigh. Severed his femoral artery and he bled out.'

'What about the sheriff?' Early asked, pointing with his

chin at the body by the front door.

'Shot three times in the head and neck.'

Early shook his head.

'Busy day for the Bucket,' Jones said.

Early stared at him flatly.

'I mean, it's on the way,' Jones said.

Early went to Kapnick's body and hunkered down in front of his boss. His skin was flaccid and his jaw and face swollen and misshapen from the effects of his injuries. His shirt was entirely soaked in blood.

Early shook his head, thinking: *this is what men do.*

82

Marshall had gone to the reception desk of the motel not long after Jimmy left the room. The girl was there alone. Marshall stood outside the door watching her leaning on the counter reading a magazine. She looked up and saw him. Marshall smiled and pushed the door open.

'Hey, our TV's not working. Can you come help?'

He said it in a rush, a rehearsed line that he had determined was unthreatening. He felt his neck flush red and hoped that it did not show.

The girl frowned at him.

'Um, I'm the only one here, you know. I mean, I don't think I can leave the desk.'

That kind of took Marshall by surprise. He had not prepared for anything other than an enthusiastic yes.

'But…it's not working,' was all that he could manage, smiling again.

'I don't know anything about fixing TVs,' she said, sounding bored.

Marshall felt frustration rising in him. He didn't know what else to say and shrugged at her.

The girl looked at her magazine, flipped it shut and said that she guessed she could have a quick look at it.

'But I'll probably need to call the owner.'

'Sure.'

Marshall pulled the door and held it open for her. He thought that would make him look good, like he was a nice guy. He felt that he was a nice guy most of the time.

The girl came around the counter and walked past Marshall. He smelled her perfume as she passed by. It was a strong, musky scent that he did not particularly like.

'Just up here,' he said, walking past her to the room.

It was all he could do to stop himself from grabbing her and pushing her into the room. Instead, he again held the door open for her.

The girl went into the room and immediately saw her mistake. The TV was on and working fine.

Marshall followed her in and closed the door.

83

Jimmy looked at his watch when he got to the motel parking lot and saw that he had been gone for maybe a half hour. He slowed to a walk and dug his hand into the pocket where he had stuffed the cash. He took it out and counted it, unaware that the same police cruiser that he had seen twice before passed behind him and came to a stop at the entrance to the lot.

The two cops watched Jimmy walk to his room and knock on the door. The cop in the passenger seat picked up the car radio mike and spoke into it, relaying the name of the motel and the room number. The information was acknowledged briefly. The cops waited, still watching Jimmy as he knocked on the door again.

'It's him, right?' the driver said.

His partner nodded and said that, yeah, it did look like him.

'Be advised,' a voice from the radio said, 'suspects are armed and considered extremely dangerous. Do not engage alone. Wait for back-up. Copy?'

The cop keyed the send button on the radio mike.

'Copy that. You calling in the Feds?'

'Copy. The FBI has been notified.'

The cop hooked the mike onto the radio and watched as the door to the room was opened and Jimmy disappeared inside.

Jimmy stopped as Marshall closed the door behind him. The room was a mess with bed covers strewn on the floor and a lamp smashed in the corner next to Marshall's bed. He saw what looked like a streak of blood on the carpet at the bathroom door. The door was closed but he could see that the light was on.

Jimmy looked at his brother. Marshall would not make eye contact. Instead, he stared at the bathroom door and lifted a hand to his mouth to bite at the nail of his index finger. His hand was spotted with blood.

Jimmy went to his brother and grabbed both arms, turning Marshall to face him.

'What happened, Marshall?'

His brother shook his head, still biting at his nail.

'It's okay,' Jimmy said, trying to keep his voice even. 'Tell me what's up.'

Marshall's eyes flicked to Jimmy's and then back to the bathroom door.

'She didn't…'

Jimmy looked over his shoulder at the stain on the carpet. When he looked at Marshall again his brother shook his head vigorously.

'I'm going to take a look in the bathroom,' Jimmy told him.

'She's still in there,' Marshall said.

'Who's in there?'

Marshall nodded but said nothing. Jimmy released his grip on Marshall's arms. His brother rubbed at them where Jimmy's fingers had dug hard into the muscle.

Jimmy was startled by a loud knock at the door. Marshall's head whipped around to the source of the noise. Jimmy held a hand up telling Marshall to stay put and stay quiet.

'Hey,' a male voice sounded from outside. 'Is everything okay in there?'

Jimmy went to the door and looked through the peephole. There was a short, fat guy in a t-shirt and a pair of shorts. Jimmy did not recognise him.

The guy banged hard on the door.

'Is anybody hurt?' he said loudly.

Jimmy watched him but said nothing. He knew now that they would have to get out of there tonight.

The guy at the door was about ten seconds from getting pulled into the room and pistol whipped when he banged once more on the door and walked away. Jimmy heard another door nearby close. He figured the guy was a guest and had heard the noise of whatever had gone on in the room.

'We need to get out of here, Marshall.'

'I don't know.'

'You don't know what?'

'She's still in there.'

Jimmy did not want to look in the bathroom. He suddenly felt very tired.

'She's still in there,' Marshall said again.

The two sheriff department cruisers were now parked across the street maybe a hundred feet apart, blocking off the road adjacent to Kapnick's house. The Bucket and the ambulance were parked at the kerb, with the ambulance lights flashing as the crew prepared to go back on shift. There was nothing more for them to do here. It was now up to Arnett Bain, who was crouched by Polite's body. A congealing river of blood ran from Polite's body, under Kapnick's car and down to the street. It looked black in the light from the street lamps. Kapnick's body was covered by a heavy-duty body bag. Early had asked Bain to do it out of respect for the man. No matter what he had done, he was still the town sheriff. There was no evidence to preserve given the events of the evening. Both combatants were dead so no charges would be brought.

Early's phone rang. He took it from the pouch on his belt and walked to the edge of Kapnick's property.

'This is Deputy Simms.'

'Special Agent Carlsson,' the woman on the other end of the phone said. 'Look, I know it's been a long day for you, but I thought it was only right that I told you we think we've identified the Cain brothers. Some local cops in Hyannis have eyes on them at a motel. We're en route ourselves right now.'

Early pinched the bridge of his nose. He decided not to tell Carlsson about Kapnick right now. She had to keep a clear focus if she was going to engage with the men responsible for what happened at the Applegate house.

'You need any back-up?' Early asked, watching Bain and his assistant unfurl another body bag for Polite.

'You don't have to do that. I mean, we'll be there along with the local cops.'

'I have a feeling that with those guys you might need as many able bodies as you can muster. That's why you called me, right? There are no more agents down here right now.'

'You're part of the task force.'

'I finish what I start. Text me the address and I'll be there in twenty minutes.'

'You'll be there before we are. Don't start anything without us, deputy.'

Early thought that she was trying too hard to sound flip about what was likely to be a serious armed engagement. What she sounded was scared, which was how she should sound.

Early said thanks and ended the call. He walked down to the sidewalk where Frank Wood and Randy Jones were standing together, not talking.

'I have to go somewhere,' he told them. 'You guys can finish up here without me.'

Wood looked at Jones and they both shrugged.

'You want we should call the state detective bureau?' Jones asked.

'To do what?'

'I don't know.'

'I think you have your answer right there, Randy. Call me if you need anything.'

Both men watched Early walk to his car. The light bar on the roof flashed to life as Early peeled away, his siren whooping as he reached the end of the street.

'Some help over here,' Arnett Bain shouted at the two deputies as he struggled with Polite's body. 'We landed a big one tonight.'

Jones looked at the younger deputy and inclined his head

towards Bain. Wood sighed and walked towards the ME.

85

'We're leaving, now,' Jimmy told his brother as he heaved the bag with the shotgun in it over his shoulder.

Marshall looked uncertainly from Jimmy to the bathroom. Jimmy ignored his brother and checked again that the magazine in the handgun was full. He put it in the waistband of his jeans at the small of his back.

'Let's go,' he said.

Marshall looked at Jimmy and nodded.

'She'll be okay in there alone, won't she?'

Jimmy said that she would be fine, the muscles of his jaw bunching as he ground his teeth together. He was good with not ever knowing what happened in here and what the interior of the bathroom looked like.

He went to the front door and pulled it open, looking back and waiting for Marshall to go outside. He pulled the door closed hard and walked forward, thinking that they would catch a bus along the road. The bag felt heavy so he pushed it further up onto his shoulder, the nylon strap tight at the juncture of his shoulder and neck.

Sergeant John Rayner of the local PD had been on his way home when he got the call about the sighting at the motel. He had pulled a quick u-turn and gunned his police cruiser towards Main Street, only a few minutes away from the motel. He called his wife on the way there, telling her that he had forgotten something and had to go back in. She had sighed. Rayner heard the sound of their newborn son crying loudly in the background and wished he was home. But he could not leave his less experienced men out there on the street if it really was the Cain brothers that had been spotted.

He approached the motel and saw the other police car parked just past the entrance. The driver waved at him to stop, but Rayner misunderstood. Thinking that he had been waved on through, Rayner kept going before turning sharply into the parking lot of the motel. He pushed down hard on his brake pedal when he saw the two men in front of him. The car slewed left and came to a stop facing diagonally on to the men, about twenty feet from them.

Jimmy dropped the bag from his shoulder, reached around and pulled the handgun from his jeans. He took aim at the cop car just as it started to reverse, the driver zig-zagging away from them.

Jimmy fired at the car. He missed with a couple of shots, but at least two connected with the windshield, spider web cracks appearing on the glass.

Jimmy reached down into the bag and pulled out the shotgun, handing his handgun to Marshall. He shouldered the shotgun and fired twice at the car as it bounced out of the lot and onto the road. The driver kept going into the McDonald's car park and crunched hard into an SUV parked there.

Another cop car pulled into sight, stopping at the entrance to the lot and blocking it to any further traffic. The two cops inside scrambled out of the car on the side facing away from Jimmy and Marshall. Jimmy put a hand across Marshall's chest and started walking backwards. Marshall raised his gun and fired at the cop cars until the hammer clicked on empty. A series of holes punctured the metal of the car and the rear passenger window shattered.

'Let's go,' Jimmy shouted, grabbing his brother's shirt and pulling him back towards the motel.

Jimmy headed for the main office, sprinting ahead of

Marshall and kicking the door open. He kept going, past the reception desk and towards a heavy fire exit door at the back. It was the kind with a metal push bar across it. Jimmy kicked the bar and the door swung open onto a narrow service yard. Beyond the yard was a sparse wooded area.

Marshall came through the fire exit door and Jimmy pushed it shut. He held the shotgun across his chest and ran into the wooded area. It looked like people maybe used the woods as a shortcut because there was a path of sorts – no more than tramped down dirt. He heard a growing chorus of sirens around them.

Rayner got out of his car and ran to the police cruiser that blocked the entrance to the motel.

'You men okay?' he asked.

The two younger cops nodded, both of them breathing hard.

'I think they went into the main office,' Rayner said. 'Does that have a back door?'

'Yeah. I mean, I think so.'

'Shit. Okay, you men go down there and secure the front of the office. Do not go inside.'

They both nodded at Rayner as another cruiser came roaring up the street.

'Get going,' Rayner shouted at the two men.

They rose from their crouched position behind the car and ran towards the motel with their handguns drawn. Rayner turned to the two officers that had just arrived. He knew that the woods behind the motel would lead the Cain brothers to a small residential area of three parallel streets – Ohio Way, Sawgrass Street and Long Way. He also knew the detail of the crimes that those men were wanted for and tried not to think of the damage they could wreak in his town.

'Turn back around and head down Long Way,' he said, leaning down to speak to the driver of the car.

After that, he ran back to his own car and radioed in that the suspects were on foot and at large in the area around the three streets.

'All cars proceed with caution. These guys are going to try to shoot their way out.'

86

Early reached the town limits of Hyannis and pulled in to the side of the road. He called 911, explained who he was and that he was there to provide whatever assistance he could.

'Can you patch me into your comms system?' he asked the operator. 'Just an open channel.'

Early thought that he was better to hear everything, no matter how confusing that may be.

'I can do that, deputy. Please hold.'

Early waited while he was put on hold. He looked at his watch. It had been more than twenty minutes since he had left Kapnick's house. Noise filled his ear as the connection to the local radio system kicked in. Early pulled his phone away from his ear and activated the speaker. He sat the phone in its holder on his dashboard, turning the volume up as high as it would go.

He heard references to street names but they meant nothing to him. He did not know the town that well. He had already entered the motel into the car's GPS and decided that he would be best to head for that location. There would no doubt be cops already on scene.

Jimmy crouched behind the fence of the last house at the south end of a row of houses. There were lights on upstairs. He was breathing heavily and felt sweat slick on his forehead. His immediate thought was to boost a car. They were not going to get far on foot with the cops out in force.

Marshall sat on the ground with his back against the fence. Jimmy did not think that he looked fully engaged in the situation in which they found themselves. He told Marshall to stay put while he went for a look at the street in front of the houses. Marshall showed no sign of acknowledging his brother. Jimmy ran at a crouch around the end of the boundary of the house and turned towards the street.

There were two cars in the driveway of the house and plenty of others parked along the street. Jimmy stayed low behind the fence and watched the street for any sign of movement. It was fully dark now, though the streetlights provided plenty of illumination. Jimmy knew that they did not have the luxury of either choice or time. The faster they moved, the better the chance that they could get out of there. He ran back to Marshall and told him that they had to go now. Marshall nodded and followed him back to the street.

The entrance to the motel was blocked by two local PD cruisers. Early saw another one in the car park of a McDonald's restaurant, resting against an SUV. There was a bunch of cops milling around behind the two cars. Early pulled in and stopped. A man almost the same height as Early approached and Early saw the sergeant's insignia on his uniform.

'Can I help you deputy?'

Early told him why he was there in as few words as he could manage.

'I'm here to help, sergeant. What can I do?'

The man looked back at the group of mostly younger cops by the cars.

'You say the Feds are on the way?' he asked as he turned back to Early.

'Two agents.'

'That's not much.'

Early did not feel the need to embellish the Sergeant's accurate take on the situation.

'What's the situation here?' Early asked.

'The two suspects opened fire on me as I approached the motel. That's my car over there.'

He pointed at the McDonald's car park.

'They then engaged another cruiser before retreating back to the main office of the motel. I have two men down there now but I think maybe they went out back into the woods.'

'I heard some chatter on your radio system on the way here. There's a residential neighbourhood back there, is that correct?'

The sergeant nodded.

'I sent two cars there.'

'You want me to go?'

'That would be great, yes.'

'Tell me where.'

Jimmy told Marshall to wait behind the fence of the last house on the street. He went quickly to the cars sitting in the driveway but they were locked and little red lights flashed inside telling him that they were alarmed. Probably had immobilisers too. He wanted an early model car, something easy. He looked up the street and saw an old VW Beetle.

'Let's go, Marshall,' he called out.

They walked along the street quickly and reached the Beetle. The doors were locked so Jimmy used the butt of the shotgun to break the window behind the driver's seat. He reached through the open window and unlocked the car.

'Jimmy…' Marshall said.

Then his brother was shooting.

Jimmy jerked upright and brought the shotgun to bear. A police car was coming down the street. Jimmy fired, racked the slide and fired again. He did it twice more. Marshall kept firing alongside him. The windscreen of the car broke apart. Jimmy saw splashes of red against the glass.

The car kept coming for a moment, then it swerved

sharply and crunched into the side of a Ford Sedan at the bottom of a driveway on the other side of the street.

Jimmy heard another noise from the bottom end of the street. He swivelled with the shotgun still held to his shoulder. There was a second cop car there. Both cops were out and crouched behind their doors. The sound of the gunfire had masked their approach. Both cops opened fire with their handguns. Jimmy stood tall and returned fire. He saw one of them go down.

The other cop fired again.

Marshall grunted beside Jimmy and fell back against the Beetle. Jimmy glanced at his brother and saw that the skin on top of his head had been peeled back where the bullet had entered Marshall's skull.

Jimmy walked forward, firing at the remaining cop as he went. When he reached the front of the car, the cop tried to run to the rear. Jimmy shot him in the back.

87

Early had his window open as he drove fast towards the junction with Long Way. He heard the distant *pop-pop-pop* of gunfire.

The junction came upon him sooner than he had expected. Early braked hard and swung his car onto the street, his rear wheel bumping against the kerb before the car straightened. The sound of gunfire had stopped. The road stretched ahead of him with the entrance to Sawgrass Street on his right. It was a simple, blue-collar neighbourhood.

Early decided to turn onto Sawgrass. He cut the corner still travelling fast. There was a police cruiser on his left resting against another car and another cruiser at the bottom of the street with its light bar flashing. Early leaned forward with his chin almost on the steering wheel and saw bodies on the ground next to the car.

The glass of the windscreen on Early's car splintered and Early winced as something tore at the top of his left arm and shoulder. He saw blood stain his uniform and felt the lack of coordination in his arm. He knew he had been shot and looked for the source of it. He saw a man leaning on the bonnet of a VW Beetle. Early's vehicle was almost parallel to that car. Early wrenched the wheel over and his cruiser ploughed into the old Beetle. The older car was no match for the power and weight of his. It spun on impact and mounted the sidewalk before crashing into a low wall at the front of a house.

Early was up and out of his car fast, smoothly drawing his sidearm and training it on the man lying on the lawn of the house where the Beetle had been parked. His left arm felt useless so he let it hang by his side. The streetlights threw awkward shadows across the scene and Early felt broken glass crunch underfoot.

'Police,' he screamed at the man. 'Stop right there.'

Jimmy Cain knew for certain that his leg was broken. The impact of the police car with the Beetle had spun the Beetle, the rear fender clipping his leg and sending him sprawling.

The big cop from the car was moving around his vehicle now with his weapon drawn. Jimmy squirmed onto his side looking for the shotgun. It was two feet away. He rolled towards it as pain spiked in his leg.

The man on the lawn rolled to his left. Early fired at him. Dirt kicked up where his bullets impacted the ground. The man reached out and Early now saw the shotgun that he was grabbing for. Early stopped moving to better plant his feet to take aim.

Jimmy got both hands on the shotgun, sat upright and brought the gun up, racking the slide to put a shell into the firing chamber of his weapon.

Early shot the man four times from less than fifteen feet. He heard a grunt as the man fell backwards, dropping the shotgun.

Early walked slowly forward with his gun still aimed at the prone man. He heard doors open along the street and raised voices.

'Police,' Early shouted. 'Get back inside, now.'

Early reached the man. He kneeled beside him and holstered his weapon. The man did not move. Early tried pulling the man onto his front with his one good arm but he could not do it. The man felt flat and heavy to Early, like he was out cold. Early put a finger to his neck, feeling for a pulse. There was none. He put his hand under the man's head and turned his face. It looked like one of the Cain brothers. Early was not sure which one.

Early stood and looked around, seeing the body of the other Cain brother about fifteen feet away, not far from the wreck of the Beetle. He could tell even from this distance that he was dead.

Early felt his head swim and sat heavily next to the body of the man he had shot. Sirens wailed in the near distance.

'One dead, one in critical condition and two others with serious gunshot wounds,' Agent Carlsson told Early, reciting the casualty list for the Hyannis PD.

They were standing outside the police department headquarters after midnight. The other agent, Keller Parrish, was inside trying to make sense of the night's events. Early's left arm was in a sling. The blast from Jimmy Cain's shotgun had broken his collarbone but had done no other serious damage that a few sutures had not been able to mend. Carlsson was smoking and Early noticed that after she took a draw from the cigarette she then held it down by her side, underneath her hand. He had seen that many times, usually young kids learning to smoke out back of the school and shielding the butt from any prying eyes. He wondered if Agent Carlsson had picked up the habit at a young age.

Early said nothing about the list of casualties.

'I heard about Kapnick,' Carlsson said after a moment of silence.

'I figured you would.'

Carlsson shook her head at it all.

'Is this the end of it?' she asked.

'We both know that it never ends.'

Carlsson took a long draw on the cigarette before dropping it to the ground and grinding it under her shoe.

'You don't need to stay here tonight, you know,' she said. 'I can get someone to drive you back. I mean, we got your statement already and we'll write it up. It's not your jurisdiction and you don't need to worry about the paperwork.'

'It all comes down to that, right? I mean, filling in the correct form and filing it all away.'

'It's the job,' Carlsson shrugged.

Early held out his hand and Carlsson grasped it firmly.

'You take care, Agent Carlsson,' he told her.

89

'Is it Tuesday?' Charlie Simms asked the man that came to his table in the sunroom and started clearing away the breakfast dishes.

It had been more than three weeks since the deaths of the Cain brothers.

'Yes, it is, Mr Simms.'

'My son comes to see me on Tuesdays.'

'That's nice.'

'He plays football. Gonna be a star.'

'He sounds like a fine boy, sir.'

Charlie Simms nodded in satisfaction. He was sitting at his favourite table looking out onto the lawn. A man in a pair of grey work pants and shirt was cutting the grass. The windows were open and the smell of cut grass permeated the room. It was a warm day.

Behind Charlie, a man as tall as he was came into the room. This man held the door open for a moment and a woman followed him into the room. She moved slowly and deliberately in the manner of someone who had recently suffered great pain and was scared that if she moved too fast that pain would return. Her hand went to her abdomen where she held it gently against the scar tissue under her lightweight blouse.

The man clearing Charlie Simms' table saw the couple and nodded at them.

'You got visitors, Mr Simms,' he said, taking the last of

the dirty dishes from the table.

'Is it my son?' Charlie asked, a wide grin spreading across his face.

The man looked at Early Simms for an answer to the question. Early shook his head.

'See for yourself,' the man told Charlie before leaving the room.

Kate Foley held onto Early's arm with her free hand as they approached Charlie's table. Charlie turned to see both of them, his smile quickly fading. Early was learning not to feel the pain that accompanied his father's disappointment.

Early pulled a chair out for Kate and she lowered herself into it slowly. Her shorts were a little loose at the waist and her face was thinner than it had been the last time that she had been here to visit.

'Hello, Mr Simms,' she said. 'How are you today?'

He looked at her intently for a moment and then slid a hand across the table to grasp one of hers.

'Is Early coming today?'

Kate looked up at Early who stood beside her impassively.

'I'm sure he'll be here,' she said.

'How's your dad?' Charlie asked.

Kate said that her dad was fine, though she was again unsure if Charlie knew to whom he was talking. She did not mention that her father was still in hospital recovering from wounds that would afflict him for the rest of his life.

Early went to a nearby table and pulled a chair over to sit beside Kate. He was in uniform, ready for another day in the line of duty.

Charlie's eyes flicked between Early and Kate and a frown furrowed his brow. He pulled his hand away from Kate, sat back in his chair and looked out into the garden. Kate put her hand on top of Early's and squeezed.

A tear slipped down Charlie Simms' cheek. He made no move to wipe it away. Early wanted more than anything to be back on his porch with the dad that he used to know, drinking beer and not talking after another hard day working on the cabin. But that would never happen again. That man, that proud, strong man was no more.

'Do you think you'll live to be as old as me?' Charlie Simms asked.

He turned from the window and looked at Early. His gaze was steady and clear. Early did not know how to answer the question. Charlie looked down at the badge on Early's breast pocket. It read 'Sheriff Simms'.

Early followed his father's gaze and realised that he too had once been Sheriff Simms. He wondered if such confusion would be too much for the man.

'Look at that,' Early said. 'We have the same name.'

'What are you talking about,' Charlie said. 'Course we got the same name. You're my son.'

Kate squeezed Early's hand hard.

'You need me at the house today?' Charlie asked. 'Still got that porch to finish, you know.'

Early leaned forward, cupped his hand on his father's neck and kissed his forehead. He sat back and smiled.

'What was that for?' Charlie Simms asked his son.

'You come on by later, Dad. I got beer in the fridge.'

THE END

24204309R00170

Printed in Great Britain
by Amazon